LOKI'S CHRISTMAS STORY
The Highland Clan, Book 11
Copyright © 2017 by Keira Montclair

This is a work of fiction. Names, characters, places and incidents are either the product of the author's imagination or are used fictitiously, and any resemblance to actual persons, living or dead, business establishments, events or locales is entirely coincidental.

Printed in the USA.

Cover Design and Interior Format

© KILLION
THE
GROUP. INC.

Loki's Christmas Story

THE HIGHLAND CLAN ELEVEN

KEIRA MONTCLAIR

NOVELS BY KEIRA MONTCLAIR

&

&

JAKE–Book Four
ASHLYN–Book Five
MOLLY–Book Six
JAMIE AND GRACIE– Book Seven
SORCHA–Book Eight
KYLA–Book Nine
BETHIA–Book Ten

&

THE SOULMATE CHRONICLES
#1 TRUSTING A HIGHLANDER

&

THE SUMMERHILL SERIES-
CONTEMPORARY ROMANCE
#1–ONE SUMMERHILL DAY
#2–A FRESH START FOR TWO

&

REGENCY
THE DUKE AND THE DRESSMAKER

THE GRANTS AND RAMSAYS

IN 1280S

GRANTS

LAIRD ALEXANDER GRANT and wife, MADDIE
John (Jake) and wife, Aline
James (Jamie) and wife, Gracie
Kyla
Connor
Elizabeth
Maeve

BRENNA GRANT and husband, QUADE RAMSAY
Torrian (Quade's son from his first marriage) and wife, Heather—Nellie and son, Lachlan
Lily (Quade's daughter from his first marriage) and husband, Kyle—twin daughters, Lise and Liliana
Bethia
Gregor
Jennet

ROBBIE GRANT and wife, CARALYN
Ashlyn (Caralyn's daughter from a previous relationship) and husband, Magnus
Gracie (Caralyn's daughter from a previous relationship) and husband, Jamie
Rodric (Roddy)
Padraig

BRODIE GRANT and wife, CELESTINA
Loki (adopted) and wife, Arabella—sons, Kenzie
and Lucas
Braden
Catriona
Alison

JENNIE GRANT and husband, AEDAN CAM-
ERON
Riley
Tara
Brin

RAMSAYS

QUADE RAMSAY and wife, BRENNA GRANT
(see above)

LOGAN RAMSAY and wife, GWYNETH
Molly (adopted) and husband, Tormod
Maggie (adopted)
Sorcha
Gavin
Brigid

MICHEIL RAMSAY and wife, DIANA
David
Daniel

AVELINA RAMSAY and DREW MENZIE
Elyse
Tad
Tomag
Maitland

CHAPTER ONE

The Scottish Highlands, 1280s

L OKI BOLTED UP IN HIS bed, panting.
His wife Arabella, heavy with their second
child, whispered, "What is it?"

"Naught. I thought I heard something. 'Tis
naught. Go back to sleep, Bella." Not one to lie
often, he hid his face when he told this bold false-
hood. Then he leaned over and planted a kiss on
her forehead.

She rolled over and sighed, closing her eyes.

He breathed a sigh of relief, not wanting to
worry her with the truth. He'd been bothered by
haunting dreams ever since they'd discovered she
was carrying again. The source of the dreams was
a mystery to him. He'd never been happier. He
adored their wee son, Lucas, and their adopted son,
Kenzie, and the work he'd poured into building his
clan was greatly satisfying.

And yet the dream kept coming. At first it had
only troubled him once every moon, but now that
Bella's time drew near, it awoke him at least once a
sennight, maybe more.

The last one had only been two days ago.

Each time he had the dream, a little more was

revealed.

It always started the same way. An old man wearing a brat of thick furs, his hood covering most of his face, would try to speak to him. Something about this stranger terrified him, and he would feel compelled to put as much distance between them as possible. In the past, he'd never actually heard the old man speak.

This time was different.

"Why are you called Loki, lad?"

Och, he hated that question. It brought back all his old fears about not belonging. Loki was not a Gaelic name, yet his birth mother had been Gaelic, and so was his adoptive family, the Grants.

Loki had been abandoned, left to die, in the middle of the forest when he was less than six summers. For the longest time, he'd had no memory of his life before beyond that he was called Loki and had no parents. He'd lived in a crate behind an inn in Ayr.

Years later, he'd encountered Brodie Grant, which he still considered the most fortunate thing to ever happen to him. After they fought together in the Battle of Largs, the man had adopted him and welcomed him into Clan Grant.

Loki had worked hard for his new clan, so much so he'd been awarded and made laird of his own castle. Alexander Grant was still his chieftain and his warriors fought for Clan Grant, but he worked his own land, something rare in the Highlands. Though the land was not as fertile as Grant land, they grew much of their own food and had a good herd of sheep that expanded every year and a loch full of fish. He'd named it Castle Curanta, meaning brave and heroic, and he did aught he could to continue making the Grants proud.

Still, the past haunted him. Over the years he'd learned the truth about his parentage. His mother's husband, the cruel bastard Edward Blackett, was not his sire. Nor was Blackett the sire of the babe Loki's mother had died delivering. Loki and his sister, Heather, now the wife of Torrian Ramsay, were the product of a loving relationship between their mother and another man, a priest. Only they'd been torn away from their true sire after their mother's death.

The name Loki? He still had no idea why or when he'd been given it.

His mother had christened him Lucas.

Shaking the thoughts away, Loki climbed out of bed, grabbed a plaid to wrap around his waist, and headed down the stairs to the great hall. True, it was small in comparison to the Grant's, but it was their own, and Bella had worked hard to make it warm and cozy. He grabbed a goblet of mead and sat in one of the chairs in front of the hearth, the fire now nothing but hot embers.

What time was it? He had no idea.

After his second swig, he heard a noise from the lads' chamber. He tipped his head toward the staircase, listening to see which of the lads had awakened. Kenzie, almost nine summers, came flying across the balcony and down the staircase.

"Papa, Papa…"

Loki stood up to greet his son, the lad who he'd found living on the streets of Ayr just as he had so many years ago. "What is it, Kenzie?"

"Papa, I keep having the same dream. I do not

like it. How do I make it stop?"

A chill ran up his spine, causing a tingling in his neck he did not like. "Sit down, lad. Tell me about it."

Kenzie fell into the chair next to him, landing on the soft cushion Bella had made and grabbing the fur tossed over the back of the chair.

Loki measured the fear in the lad's gaze, watching to see if it grew or if it banked like the fire had. "Lad, it seems so real, aye?" he whispered, hoping his voice would calm the boy.

Kenzie rubbed the sleep from his eyes. "A big man. 'Tis a large man every time. He's all covered in furs, and he asks me questions."

"What does he say?" He wasn't sure he wished to hear the lad's answer, because the similarities were already unnerving.

"One time he said, 'Where's my Loki?' Another time he asked me why my papa was named Loki. His questions made me think of my true papa. I'd love him, too, if he were still alive. Can I not love both my papas? Do you think 'tis why the man with the furs is after me?" He hopped out of his chair and stood directly in front of Loki, his eyes wide and misting.

"Nay, I do not think he is after you."

"But I can love two papas, can I not? Does it bother you that I still love my first papa?"

"Nay, it does not bother me. I'm pleased you love two papas. I love four if the truth be known." He grinned at Kenzie, hoping to pull the lad's fear from him by distracting him with a puzzle. He was easy to distract at the tender age of nine summers.

"Four? You love four papas?"

"Can you not guess who I mean?" He leaned back in his chair, giving the lad a chance to think it through. Kenzie was certainly bright enough to figure out the answer.

"Your true papa, the priest, and Grandsire Brodie, your adopted sire. Hmmm…"

Loki smiled, watching his son's expression change as the thoughts bounced around in his head.

"I know. Uncle Alex."

"Aye, 'tis the third. And the fourth?"

His chest plumped out in satisfaction, but it fell back down as soon as he remembered he had to come up with one more.

"Uncle Robbie?"

"Aye. They all treated me like their son when I arrived here. I'm blessed beyond words."

"I am, too, Papa." He threw his arms around Loki's neck.

"I'll tell you a secret."

Kenzie propelled himself away from Loki's chest. "A secret? Do tell."

"I've had my own dreams about the man in the furs."

"You have? Does he scare you, too?"

How to lie about this one… He was more frightened than ever now that he knew they were having similar dreams, but the truth would alarm his son. He settled on a half-truth.

"The man in the furs scares me when it's dark, but as soon as daylight arrives, he vanishes. Think on that, and he'll not be able to scare you again."

"I'll try, Papa. I hope it works. But who is the man in the furs?"

That was the strangest thing of all. Loki had no idea.

CHAPTER TWO

TWO NIGHTS LATER, LOKI LAY awake in his bed, staring up at the beams in his bed chamber with his hands behind his head. Bella tossed and turned, something that had become more frequent in the later part of her pregnancy. Though he loved Lucas and Kenzie, Loki couldn't help but hope they'd have a wee lassie this time. Poor Bella's house was overrun with lads.

Loki had been awakened by another dream of the man in furs. This time he'd asked, "Where are you, Loki? I need you."

He'd awakened in a cold sweat, but he'd decided not to move about for fear of awakening Bella. Still no closer to understanding the meaning of the man in furs, he couldn't sleep. Kenzie hadn't complained about any more dreams, but only a couple of nights had passed.

Bella rolled over and stared at him. The dark made it hard to see, but the look on her face told him that if it were daylight, he'd see that gleam in her eyes he loved so much.

She gave him a sweet smile, and he knew exactly what was on her mind.

"Restless, my wee one?" he asked.

"Wee one? Who do you think you're talking to,

husband?" She rolled onto her back and tossed the covers off, pulling up her night rail to expose her belly. "Does that look wee to you, because I think not."

He laughed and rolled onto his side, leaning over to capture her lips with his own, delving into her sweet mouth with his tongue. "Are you trying to torture me, lass? You know I cannot climb aboard you at this point."

She laughed and drawled, "Mayhap 'tis my turn to enjoy the climbing."

"I'm all yours." He kissed her again and his hand crept down to the vee between her legs. "I see you've been thinking on me, aye?"

She pushed against his chest until he was flat on his back, grinning. She loomed over him and said, "I'll show you how much I've been thinking on you." Bella lifted her leg to straddle him and he grabbed her hips, guiding her to the right place. She began to ride him, the friction immediately making him hard, but then almost toppled off of him.

"Whoa, lassie, you'll not be leaving me after starting that." He repositioned her and said, "Hold on to my hands. I'll keep you just where you want to be."

Bella grabbed his hands to anchor herself, then began to writhe her mound against him. It didn't take long until she lifted herself, panting, and took him inside, sheathing him completely with a deep sigh and a moan. "Loki, I do love you so."

"Come for me, my Bella."

She moved while he pleasured her every way he could.

"Your breasts are so full and beautiful. I love holding them." As he caressed them and tweaked her nipples, he felt her sheath tighten around him. She let go with a moan and he followed, climaxing with her.

When they finished, he helped her into a position next to him, her head on his shoulder and her belly braced on his hip. "You must have wanted me," he said. "You sure went fast, love."

She giggled. "Happens every time you call this big body beautiful."

"You know 'tis only the bairn making you big, and you are still beautiful."

A loud knock interrupted their intimacy, though they were fortunate it had not come a moment or two sooner.

"Come in," Loki shouted after he helped Bella settle her gown, afraid it was Kenzie again. He pulled the covers up past his waist.

Kenzie bounded inside and threw himself across the bed.

"What is it, Kenzie?"

They didn't have to wait long for his answer. Words spilled out of his mouth as fast as a falcon diving after its prey. "The man with furs came again. Make him stop, Papa. Make him go away. He scares me. I hate him. I…"

"Slow down, lad. You have not taken a breath after five sentences. You had another dream about the man in the furs?" He'd told Bella a bit about the dreams that had been plaguing him and Kenzie, though not in enough detail to concern her. She was too far along to be worrying about such things.

"Aye, and he told me something this time. Now I'm more afraid than ever."

Bella moved away from Loki and motioned for Kenzie to come lie between them. "Come rest with us and tell us all about it."

He did as she asked, maneuvering his wee body between them and then rolling over onto his back.

"Good. Now take a deep breath and start anew," Bella whispered.

"The man with the furs came to me in my sleep again. This time, he told me something different." The tears slid down his cheeks as he glanced from his mama to his papa. "I could see my true sire standing behind the man of furs. 'Tis the first time I've seen him since he passed, and he did not look happy. I fear he does not want me to have two families. What have I done wrong?"

"Naught," Loki said, reaching down to ruffle the lad's hair. "You've done naught wrong, Kenzie. I do not think your true sire is upset with you. Did he say aught?"

"Nay. 'Twas the look in his eyes that worried me." He sat up and glanced from one of them to the other. "And then the man in the furs told me that I must bring you to Ayr, Papa. I think my true papa must want it, too, or he would not have been there."

Bella looked at Loki, her gaze full of love, and said, "Then you must go."

❧

The next afternoon, Loki sat near the warm hearth beside Bella, his sire Brodie, and his mother Celestina. Wee Lucas was cuddled on his grandmama's lap.

Loki cleared his throat before he began. "I thank you both for coming. I know not if I'm chasing something foolish, but Kenzie is so upset by these dreams that I'm hoping he'll settle if we take him seriously. I...have to admit it troubles me that we've seen the same person in our dreams."

"And will you go as far as Ayr?" Bella asked.

"I cannot say, but I'll do my best to return as soon as I can, lassie. You know I've no desire to leave you. I'm only glad that Mama and Papa can stay with you while I'm gone. I'll take this one day at a time, see if the lad and I continue to have the dreams after we depart." He lowered his voice. "I cannot allow our son to believe 'tis wrong to love two fathers. You've seen how distraught he is."

Bella's eyes teared up right away. "I know. I've not seen him this upset before. I thought he'd get over it when the sun rose, but it has only worsened." She grasped Loki's hand and squeezed it. "Do not worry. I'll be fine."

"Poor Kenzie. I can see the worry in his face. It unsettles me, Loki." Celestina ran one hand over the sleeping bairn on her lap with a shake of her head. "Do what you must. Your brother will bring the girls over later. We'll all be here to help Bella."

"Mama, do you believe the dreams mean something?" He valued both of his parents' opinions, but he'd heard his mother discuss the significance of dreams with his aunts. It seemed likely she might know something. Besides, his adoptive mother was an angel, more ethereal than anyone he'd ever met. If any living person knew of matters beyond this world, he trusted that she did.

His mother thought for a moment, then reached for his sire's hand. "Loki, I for certes do not understand why the man asks about your name, but the fact that you've both been visited by a similar vision makes me think there is more to it."

"You're sure you've never discussed your dreams in front of him?" his father asked, glancing back and forth between him and Bella. "'Tis most unusual that you've dreamed of the same man. You know of Avelina Ramsay and her powers. There are some aspects of this world that cannot be explained. This could be one of them."

Both shook their heads in unison. He wouldn't even confess how many times he'd hidden his dreams from Bella, not wanting to worry her during her time. But he could no longer ignore them. It would seem someone had a message for him and his son.

The door leading outside flew open and Kenzie bounced down the steps toward them. "We brushed down your horses, Grandsire. You'll take good care of Mama while we're gone?" Kenzie moved over to hug Bella fiercely.

"We will. I promise you."

Kenzie stared at the floor for a moment before he whispered, "Do you think I'm daft, Grandmama? Do you think my true sire hates me for loving Mama and Papa?"

"Oh, Kenzie." She handed Lucas off to Loki and patted her lap. To everyone's surprise, the lad settled sideways on her lap, resting his head on her shoulder. "Your sire left this world too soon. He could not see you become a man, but I think he would be thrilled that you found Loki and Bella.

Love is what makes us happiest, and have you not heard that the more love you give, the more you will receive?"

Kenzie sat up to stare into his grandmother's eyes, his expression serious. "I'll have to think on that. You do not think my true sire is upset with me for loving all of you?"

"Nay. I think if he were here, he would thank us all for taking you in and loving you as though you were our verra own. We do not ask you to forget your parents, which is also important. You do not believe your parents would be pleased to think of you living alone on the streets of Ayr, do you?"

"Nay, they would not want me to live there. That is true, but I must find out for sure. And I must find out about why the man in my dreams is so interested in Papa. 'Tis strange that we're having the same dreams, is it not?"

Brodie stood up and clasped his grandson's shoulder. "Our hope is that you'll find the answers you seek quickly so you can return to your mama and help her with the new bairn."

They left the next morning.

CHAPTER THREE

❦

LOKI DECIDED TO STOP AND visit Clan Grant since they needed to travel through Grant land in order to reach the well-traveled path out of the Highlands. Every time he visited his childhood home, he was flooded with memories of the past. Happy times he'd spent running across the grounds with his cousins Jamie and Jake, playing with Torrian and his deerhound, and courting his Bella. Aunt Maddie and Uncle Alex persuaded them to stay for the night, and after dinner they gathered around the warm hearth to talk with their dear relatives.

"I hope you return in time to share in our Christmas celebration," Aunt Maddie said.

Kenzie hopped out of his chair. "We have to be back, do we not, Papa?" he asked eagerly.

Loki said, "We'll do our best as long as the storms don't keep us away. We've agreed to celebrate the solstice here and at Castle Curanta. We also must consider 'tis possible Bella could bring this new bairn into the world around the winter solstice. You know I cannot miss that, nor would you like to miss it. Am I not correct?"

"Aye, we must be home to see the new bairn. We will have to find the man with the furs quickly,"

Kenzie said, the expression on his face clearly communicating that he had no intention of spending much time in Ayr. All the better.

"We'll do our best to wait for you, lad," Uncle Alex said.

Aunt Maddie added, "And we'll all go to Castle Curanta if Bella delivers the bairn. Caralyn's help will be needed, and we can keep one another company."

"My thanks to you both. I know Bella will appreciate the assistance, especially with wee Lucas." Loki couldn't help but worry about the timing of their trip, but he knew it would be worse to wait. Bella would be more than busy after the babe came, and travel would be dangerous once winter settled in. No, best to go ahead of the winter solstice.

Alex brought him back to their conversation, knowing just what Kenzie wished to hear. "We're hoping to have a successful hunting trip, Kenzie. At least one or two deer and a goose or two is our hope."

"Aye, Uncle Alex," the lad said, jumping up and down in excitement. "'Tis my favorite. I love venison meat pies. We must return, Papa. And fruit pies, too, Aunt Maddie?" Loki couldn't help but smile at the lad's exuberance. He himself had probably looked that way after his first experiences with the Grants and their wonderful cook. A lad who'd gone hungry many times learned to appreciate the blessings of good food.

"Of course," Maddie said with a grin. "We have many berries and apples. We will have plenty for all. We'll be sure to send a basket to your mama and grandparents if you're not back in time for the celebration. I'll give you a sack of fruit and some oatcakes to take on your trip."

"But we will be back in time. We will!" Kenzie glanced from Alex to Maddie and back. "Will you not have evergreens decorated around the hall so it smells sweet?"

"Aye, we will."

"And fresh rushes?"

"Aye."

"And big, fat loaves of bread?"

Maddie smiled. "Of course. I'll make you your own special loaf, Kenzie."

"Papa, we must return in time. We must!"

The door burst open, a gust of wind howling in behind the newest visitors. Alex and Maddie's son, Jamie, entered with his second, Finlay, and Finlay's brother Fergus. Gillie followed them in, stomping his feet for warmth. The lad, an orphan of ten and four summers, had joined Clan Grant after the clan's recent battle with the Buchans.

"Loki, what brings you to Grant land in this cold weather?" Jamie bellowed, his cheeks pink from the weather. He grinned at them with his usual good cheer.

"Och, we have an important journey to make to Ayr. Kenzie and I are looking to visit with some old friends." Loki gave Kenzie a pointed look, hoping he wouldn't talk about his dreams to all. They'd already created enough of a fuss.

"Why not take Gillie with you?" Jamie asked. "He was planning to visit you around the time of the wee bairn's arrival."

Gillie grinned. "Aye, normally I would, but I'd prefer to be here for the winter solstice after all the tales I've heard about the food. I'm heading home to help Nicol with some chores, but I wished to stop by and give greetings to you and Kenzie." He stayed for a moment, chatting with Kenzie, and then left with a wave.

As the door closed behind him, a quiet voice said, "I'd like to go with you if you'll have me." Fergus lifted his chin a notch.

Finlay shot a surprised look at his elder brother. The two had lost their mother not long ago—a loss that was still felt by all in the clan. Of the brothers, Finlay had recovered more fully from his grief. He'd married Kyla, Alex and Maddie's daughter, but Fergus still seemed lost. Perhaps it would be good for him to get out.

"Truly?" Finlay asked. "Back to Ayr? During the solstice? Why not stay and enjoy the brief holiday? 'Twill do you good."

"Aye. I know not what to say except that I'm restless. I've felt unsettled ever since we lost Mama. Loki? What say you?" Fergus didn't look at anyone else for guidance.

Loki glanced at his uncle Alex first to gauge his reaction, but as always, his uncle kept his feelings well hidden. So he took the measure of the others before he replied.

Finlay took two steps back, staying outside of his brother's view, and shook his head no.

Jamie took a step behind Finlay and nodded his head in agreement.

At last he turned to look at Aunt Maddie. He paused for a moment to reflect in her goodness, how much they all treasured her presence and guidance. Then she gave him a barely perceptible nod and a wink.

Loki said, "Pack your things. We leave at dawn, as soon as we get our bellies filled. The pickings will be random on our journey."

☾

Fergus MacNicol left the great hall with a smile on his face. He knew all too well that his brother would follow him. Sure enough, he heard the door bang shut behind him as Finlay rushed out to speak with him.

"Could your decision not have waited until we talk with Da?" Fergus peered sideways at his brother, huddled inside the wool tunic he'd worn to practice in the lists. "I know 'tis our first solstice celebration without Mama, but I don't wish to lose my brother, too." He gave a shudder, then said, "'Tis a mighty bitter wind out here today. Let's move along."

Rather than answer, Fergus pushed himself to a run toward the small cottage he and his sire and now Gillie shared inside the bailey—the same cottage where they'd lost their mother to that awful growth in her belly. Finlay broke into a run behind him.

"Why now?" his brother shouted.

"I didn't choose the timing for Loki's trip."

They arrived at the cottage and Fergus burst in through the door. His sire and Gillie were busy piling wood next to the hearth, enough to keep the building warm overnight against the cutting wind. The hut was neatly tucked into a corner not far from the curtain wall, which protected it from the worst of the wind.

As soon as they stepped inside, Finlay hurried over to their father. Between gasps of air, he said, "Fergus is leaving with Loki."

Their sire didn't even hesitate. "When is Loki leaving? And why? What are his plans?"

"He's bringing Kenzie to Ayr to visit someone. Fergus asked if he could go along. What say you, Papa?"

Nicol tossed wood into the dying embers, stirring the fire to keep it going. "From your question, I'm assuming you do not agree with Fergus's decision. Or is it Loki you disagree with?"

"I think Fergus should stay with us. 'Tis out first year without Mama. We should all be together."

"But you have Kyla." Finlay had had the good fortune of marrying his perfect match, something that had not yet happened for Fergus. At one time, he'd fancied himself in love with Gracie Grant, but now he knew they'd have never suited. Gracie and Jamie belonged together, undoubtedly.

"Aye, so Papa will be alone if you leave."

"Nay, I will not be alone." Their sire stood and turned to face them both.

"What?" Finlay asked, dumbfounded.

"This will be a difficult year for all of us. Finlay, you have a new wife, and you'll be celebrating with her family. You know how her mother fusses over the holiday, and she'll involve you in all of the Grants' plans. I couldn't be happier for you. I made this plan just the other day."

"Why?" Fergus asked, now joining his brother in curiosity.

"Since Brodie and Celestina have gone to Castle Curanta to be with Bella when the new bairn arrives, they've invited all of us to join them. Fergus, you're welcome to come if you'd like, but if you'd prefer to travel with Loki, you have my blessing." Fergus's father and Brodie Grant were lifelong friends, so it was no surprise the couple had issued such an invitation.

"You knew Loki was leaving?" Finlay pressed.

"Aye, Loki sent word to his parents to ask for their help. The Grant castle is always bustling at the holidays, and Bella will be needing help, so I said I would be happy to join them, and Gillie said he also wished to go, though perhaps he'd rather travel with the lads."

"Then I'll be here alone," Finlay stated, his hands on his hips.

"Will you?" his sire asked.

"Nay, you'll not be alone," Gillie insisted.

Finlay settled into a chair by the hearth with a whoosh. "Nay, I'll have Kyla and Jamie and Gracie and…"

"Too many to count. I couldn't be happier for you, son. Gillie did not know your mother, so he can make his own choice of where he wishes to go, but Fergus and I are alone. I had hoped he would go to Loki's with me, but if he'd prefer to travel to Ayr, then I encourage him to do so." With that, he turned to face Fergus. "Is there any special reason you're leaving? May I help in any way?"

Fergus sat at the table in the far corner. "As I explained to Finlay, I'm restless."

"You're missing your mother, as we all are. I feel exactly the same way, which is why I plan to be with my old friend for the holidays. You recall 'twas Brodie and I who found Loki hiding in the bushes in Ayr, do you not? He was a wee lad as small as his Kenzie."

Finlay nodded. After a deep sigh, he heaved himself out of the chair and made his way to the table. Clasping his brother's shoulder, he said, "Then go with my blessing, but I'll still wish you'll return by the solstice."

Gillie stood by the pile of wood, kneading his hands. "I'll stay here with your papa. Will we enjoy a feast at Castle Curanta, too? I don't wish to miss Maddie's, but I'd rather stay with you, Nicol."

"Aye, we'll have food at both places. 'Tis our tradition at the winter solstice—feast and make merry with the clan. We are close enough to travel to both eventually."

Gillie nodded emphatically. "I'll go wherever there's a celebration. I've had enough of being cold and hungry during the solstice. I have no desire to return to Edinburgh. Mayhap someday."

Nicol declared, "Fergus, go with all of our blessings. Is that not right, Finlay?"

"Aye," Finlay said, squeezing his brother's shoulder again. "I wish you a safe journey."

Fergus nodded. He wouldn't tell his brother or his sire the truth.

He needed to find the woman of his dreams.

CHAPTER FOUR

LOKI HAD HOPED FOR THE chance to talk to Gillie earlier, but there had been too many people around. A lad living in the streets was often aware of everything that happened in a burgh. Though Gillie might not know aught, he thought it wise to ask.

Before they sought their bed that night, Loki and Kenzie made their way to Nicol's cottage. When they arrived, Nicol and Gillie were the only two present, sitting at the table with hot drinks. When Nicol issued an invitation for the pair to join them, Loki sat and motioned for his son to do the same. Loki trusted his father's friend implicitly, so he didn't mind speaking openly in front of him.

"Sorry to disturb you both so late," Loki said, "but we were hoping to ask some questions of Gillie."

"Aye, what is it?" the lad asked curiously.

"You lived in Edinburgh for a while. Have you ever heard of a man who wears furs, even a hood of furs that covers his face?"

"All the way to his feet," Kenzie added, glancing sideways at his papa.

"Aye, I've seen a man like that," Gillie shrugged his shoulders, oblivious to the importance of his revelation to Kenzie and Loki.

"You have?" Kenzie bolted to his feet in a matter of seconds.

Loki gently tugged on his son's plaid until he was once again seated. "Where have you seen him and how long ago?" He did his best to hide his own excitement, especially since the wee lad expressed enough for both of them. Besides, there could very well be two such men.

"That is, if you mean the man of the bairns. He used to come to Edinburgh once every couple of moons in search of children who lived in the streets. He took them off the streets, fed them at his big cottage."

"Why didn't you go along with him?" Kenzie asked. "If he'd been in Ayr when I was there, I would have gone. Many nights it was verra cold."

"I noticed he usually took the young ones in, not any lads of my age. After the first time I saw him, I asked others about him and they said he was most reputable. I met someone who'd lived with him for a while. He took in the lost souls, that's what he called them. If you had no home and wished to eat, he was the one who'd help you. He kept around ten bairns in his cottage, all huddled together on the floor in his hut. He slept separately. He fed them and they all did chores."

"And they were warmer than I was."

"But you've no need of his help now, Kenzie. Recall why we need to find this man in the furs." Sometimes it was a challenge keeping Kenzie focused, but he tried to keep that hidden from the lad, doing his best to patiently guide him instead.

"Aye, Papa. Where is his cottage, Gillie? We'll go

talk to him."

Gillie gave them a look Loki didn't like. "I have no idea. Sorry. No one ever said where, and I never asked."

"Papa, we must go to Edinburgh instead. We're heading the wrong way."

Gillie said, "Mayhap not. They said he traveled to all the Scottish royal burghs. Gathered bairns from everywhere."

"Then we head to Ayr. Remember your dream, Kenzie? We must heed it." The others exchanged looks, but no one questioned them.

The following morning was clear, which pleased Loki. There was little he hated more than traveling in drenching rain. He'd take the snow any day over the dampness that soaked deep into your bones. His favorite part of the ride to Ayr was the stunning view it gave him of the mountains of the Highlands. Something about that expanse of beautiful, rugged land both reminded him of how small he was in comparison with nature's glory and anchored him to his adopted home. He always gave thanks when he saw that view, forever grateful for how the Grants had changed and expanded his world.

The group ended up being larger than Loki had anticipated, but since it was almost the dead of winter, it was a good idea to have extra travelers. Besides Kenzie and Fergus, he'd brought three of his own guards, and Uncle Alex had insisted on sending another five men. His uncle had claimed he was sending them just to help hunt, but Loki knew better. They all knew unrest still roiled in the Highlands after the defeat of Glenn of Buchan, the

Grants' longtime adversary. His uncle was ensuring they had protection from reivers searching for coin or wealth.

They'd almost made it to Ayr when they found a cave to settle in for the night to protect them against the wind, one large enough for the horses to huddle in just at the edge. The wind kept up a brief whistle, but the furs and shelter would keep them warm.

They allowed the horses to graze while they made a fire just at the mouth of the cave to cook the two rabbits they'd shot along the way. Fergus's skills with a bow were impressive.

They sat chewing rabbit bones around the fire, discussing their plan for the trip to Ayr.

"Are you visiting your true sire, the priest, Loki? Does he not live in Ayr?" Fergus asked.

"Aye, he lives there for most of the year, but he heads to Edinburgh every Christmas. I'll probably not see him, but I know he'll be up to visit the new bairn in the spring," Loki replied, tossing his bare rabbit bone off into the woods.

They ate in silence until Kenzie couldn't keep quiet any longer. "Papa, mayhap he's seen the man."

Loki gave him a sideways glance, then decided Fergus would probably hear about the purpose of their journey soon enough. "Fergus, you traveled around the area some during our big battle with the Buchans." Without revealing the truth about the dreams, he asked. "Have you ever heard of the man of furs?"

Fergus thought for a moment, tossed another bone out of the cave. "Nay, not that I recall," he said. "Why would you think I would know aught about him?"

Loki rolled his eyes. "You don't think I've taken notice of all your requests to travel back to Buchan and Cameron land? I'm not sure what exactly draws you there, but there's some reason a man who's never liked to leave home has volunteered three or four times to patrol the area with the Grant guards. You wish to share your true purpose for this journey? I'm glad to have you along, but it does make me curious."

"Mayhap I'm missing my mother. My brother's never around anymore. He's too busy living the happy life with Kyla."

Rather than respond, Loki merely arched his brow.

Fergus heaved a sigh. "That does not sound the way I intended. I'm happy for my brother. Truly. But it all makes me unsettled. That's the best word for it. I'm just restless." He made a point not to look Loki in the eye.

Kenzie's gaze jumped back and forth between the two men, waiting to see what would come next.

Mayhap he'd let it go…for now. But when Loki got up to head outside the cave to relieve himself, he couldn't help but cast a parting remark over his shoulder. "I'll find out who she is before we're done."

Kenzie broke into a fit of giggles.

❧

A day later, the group arrived at the toll booths outside of Ayr. Once they paid the toll, Kenzie couldn't contain his excitement. He bounced about in the saddle behind Loki. "Hurry, Papa. We must visit Woodgait. 'Tis where we both lived."

Fergus said, "I still cannot believe both of you lived alone when you were young, surviving out in the wild. I couldn't have done it."

"You'd be surprised what you can do when you have no choice," Loki said as they rode through the streets. "'Twas forced on both of us, just as it was on Gillie. And besides, 'twas not the wild, Fergus. In fact, Kenzie and I will show you exactly where we lived."

A short distance later, Kenzie shouted, "Over there."

A rush of memories filled Loki's mind as the familiarity of his surroundings wrapped around him as though welcoming him home. But he knew the truth of it well enough. Thanks to Brodie Grant, this was no longer his home.

He'd learned long ago that he had everything he needed—his clanmates, the beauty of the Highlands, and the love of his sweet Bella and their boys. Their son, Lucas, would never live in a cold crate behind an inn.

He pulled on the reins of his horse and held his hand up to indicate they were stopping. After releasing Kenzie, who quickly raced to the back of the inn, he climbed down and tied his horse's lead to a branch on the closest tree. He hoped they wouldn't find another living where the two of them had spent so much time cold, hungry, and alone.

When he caught up to Kenzie, Fergus directly behind him, they all stared at the ground littered with torn clothing. The same three crates Kenzie had kept in careful order were now haphazardly arranged.

"Papa?" Kenzie's gaze took in the scattered mess in front of him, and Loki was sure they were thinking the same thing.

A grizzled older man came around the building, approaching the group. "You looking for the lad who lived back here?"

"Aye," Kenzie said, glancing at his father for approval.

"There is a lad who has been living here?" Loki asked.

The innkeeper put his hands on his hips. "Was. There was a lad who'd been living here."

"Can you tell us more?"

The innkeeper brushed his hands together as if sending crumbs to the floor. He stared at the ground for a moment before he lifted his head to answer their question. "The poor lad became gravely ill. A man came along a couple of days ago and took the lad with him. I did not know the man, but he said he only intended to heal the boy."

"The man with furs! It must have been him! Was it not?" Kenzie had difficulty staying in one spot, instead darting from one place to another as he took in every detail of the area behind the inn.

"Aye," the innkeeper answered. "'Twas the man who visits once a year. Never here long, but he spreads hope among the young scamps. What know you of him?"

"Verra little," Loki answered. "But we are seeking the man who is covered with furs. Do you know where he was headed?"

"Aye. He left a couple of days ago, said he would

take the lad to Doongait to see if he could heal him. If not, he said he would take him home, though he never said where that would be."

"Our thanks." He nodded to the innkeeper, who turned about, shaking his head, and returned to the warmth of his inn. "Mount up, lad," he said to Kenzie. "We're headed to Doongait. Be quick now."

Loki couldn't be more pleased. If the man of furs was still in Ayr, they'd surely find him. He didn't want to tell Kenzie, but he'd had another dream the night before in the cave. The man in the furs had appeared and said to hurry.

He had no idea what that meant, but he thought it best to heed the man's word.

🌙

Fergus took his time, patrolling and scanning all of Ayr to see if he could be fortunate enough to locate the woman of his dreams, but to no avail.

It didn't matter. He was a patient man. He'd find her if it took the entire year.

Part of him had wished to confide in Loki. And yet…he knew how he would sound to others. They would think him a lovesick fool, incapable of looking at the situation objectively.

But he was. Aye, Davina of Buchan was a beautiful woman, but it wasn't simply her beauty that had turned his head. The lass had faced tragedy after tragedy and survived. Her strength humbled him, and he could think of no other woman he'd prefer as his partner.

Still, there was no denying they'd only had one encounter—a meeting at Lochluin Abbey that had

soaked down to his very soul. He'd never told anyone about it. How could he explain how badly it
had made him want her?

He'd gone back to the abbey, only to learn she'd
left a short time ago. The nuns had no knowledge
of where she'd gone. She'd only told them she was
getting a cottage of her own, somewhere close
to "home." Ayr was close to Buchan land, was it
not? Surely someone would remember her if she'd
passed through. She was so beautiful, so unique...

Of course, if he did find her, there was still the
question of whether his clan would accept her. Her
background was troubled, to say the least, and her
father and former lover had forced her to play a
key role in their attempted trick on Torrian Ramsay.

But people could change. He'd just have to convince everyone it was possible. She'd been handed
one of the worst possible scenarios, but mayhap
all of that was in the past. Mayhap it was time for
both of them to find a wee bit of happiness. There
was an innate goodness in her that had never been
allowed to bloom, and he wished more than anything to help her cultivate it.

He wasn't going back without her.

❦

As they rode to Doongait, Loki said a quick
prayer that they would find the man in furs forth-
with. He had to get home to Bella.

As soon as they arrived in Doongait, they made
their way to the nicest inn, the one the Grants
frequented whenever they traveled in the burgh.
They settled the horses in the town stable, out of

the wind, but as soon as Loki stepped outside into the fresh air, he froze.

There he was—the man in the furs. He stood not fifty paces away from him, hunched over next to a small, shivering bairn. Kenzie caught sight of him a few seconds after Loki did, and the look of horror on the wee lad's face sent a chill down Loki's spine. The strangest thing about him was they could not see his face. His hood of furs obscured his looks, just as it had in the dreams.

"I see him. Papa, 'tis the man in my dreams." Kenzie's shaking finger came up slowly to point to the man.

The man in furs lifted his hand to wave at them, as if he understood why they were there. Could he?

Fergus crept up behind them, whispering, "Is he the one?"

"Aye," Loki said. "Wait here, and I'll speak with him."

"May I come, Papa?" Kenzie asked.

Loki gave him a wave, indicating for him to follow along, only because he refused to take his eyes off this vision that had haunted his dreams for so long. They moved across the road together, and Loki found his steps slowing, as if he were afraid to discover the truth. How could he and Kenzie both have had dreams about this person they'd never met? He'd never been on Grant land, so they couldn't have encountered him there.

When they reached the man in furs' side, he finally dropped his hood.

He reached down to pat Kenzie's head and whispered, "Greetings, Kenzie."

Kenzie didn't speak, instead staring at him in awe. "We meet again, lad."

CHAPTER FIVE

L OKI HELD THE DOOR FOR the old man, peering at the wee one by the man's side. He spoke to the innkeeper, who led them to a small private dining chamber with a table for six and a warm hearth.

Loki handed the man a coin and said, "Meat pies and ale for all, and some goat's milk for the wee one if you have it." The urchin was a lass, gaunt and still shivering, who looked no older than two summers. She never spoke, just stared at them with dark circles under her eyes.

When the innkeeper left, he turned to the man in furs, as yet unnamed.

"How do you know my name?" Kenzie blurted out.

The man settled in the chair closest to the hearth, lifting the wee lass onto his lap and covering her with his furs to warm her. He lowered his hood again, revealing chubby cheeks and a full beard of a mixture of white and gray whiskers. Wrinkles covered his skin where it was visible, and his kind eyes were a shade of gray unlike anything Loki had ever seen before.

Once they were all seated, the man replied, "I had hoped to see you again someday. We met, och, mayhap two summers ago. You were a new one in the land of orphans, and I offered to take you home with me, just as I'll do with this wee one on my lap."

"But I don't remember you," Kenzie declared, clearly frustrated by this piece of news.

"Who are you?" Loki asked.

Fergus stood abruptly, interrupting them. "I'll search the area, make sure we're safe here for the night. Then I'll find a place for the guards to stay."

Loki nodded, then waved him off.

"I go by many names," the man in the furs said, "but you may call me Bor. I travel to save the wee ones. 'Tis how I met Kenzie here. He took the death of his parents hard. I invited him to stay with me, but he refused. 'Twas his choice, but I wished him well."

"Bor…" Kenzie began. "But I do not ever remember speaking with you."

Loki put his hand on the lad's shoulder. "Sometimes when pain is fresh, it prevents aught from settling in your mind. You may have met him immediately after you lost your parents. The mind protects itself in odd ways." At least, he was fairly certain that was the reason he couldn't remember why his name was Loki. He'd blocked it out for some reason.

With a twinkle in his eye, Bor nodded. "I accept it if you do not remember me. We're all here together now."

"There was a lad who lived behind the inn in Woodgait, the same place my papa and I once lived," Kenzie said. "Where is he? They said he was ill."

Bor shook his head. "He is back at my cottage, healing. The cold, damp conditions were too much for him, and he was quite sick. I'm heading that direction on the morrow. I wish to get wee Ami back before it's too late for her. She needs heat."

"Ami is her name?" Loki asked. The lass was as cute as any young lass could be, though she lacked the fat needed to survive the harsh winters in their land.

As if on cue, the wee lass climbed off of Bor's lap and stepped cautiously over to Kenzie, tugging on his hand. "Does she not speak?" Kenzie asked, as he hauled the wee bairn up onto his lap.

"Nay, but she is only around two summers old. Her full name is Amice. You're young, lad. She seeks your heat, the heat that I can only give her with my furs. Wrap your arms around her to warm her."

"Where did she come from? She's too young to lose her mother," Loki said.

"I found her at the kirk. She'd wandered in and settled on one of the benches. I know not how the priest knew her name, but he did. All he could tell me was that she was English and her parents were gone."

Kenzie warmed Ami as best he could, wrapping his arms around her. She cuddled next to him, stuck her thumb in her mouth and closed her eyes.

Not long after, the innkeeper came in with a tray of meat pies along with a sweet-smelling broth full of root vegetables, goblets of ale, and goat's milk for sweet Ami. Before he left, he said, "Your sleeping chambers are ready for you, my lord." Loki thanked him and advised him they'd find him when they were ready to bed down for the night.

They all ate heartily, especially Ami, who took a special liking to the warm broth. She stayed seated between Loki and Kenzie on a tall stool the innkeeper brought in, occasionally offering them all a warm smile. Once they finished the meal, Bor looked at Kenzie and said, "I sense you have more questions for me, lad. Go ahead and I'll answer what I'm able."

Kenzie glanced at Loki, who nodded, encouraging him to ask his questions. Mayhap the end of their journey was already upon them, although Loki doubted it would be this easy.

He was certain of one thing. This was the man in *his* dreams.

Kenzie struggled to find words, but he finally met the man's eyes and said, "I have had dreams about a man in furs. Are you that man?"

Bor chuckled. "Son, there are many men who travel covered in furs this time of year. We do not all don plaids as the Highlanders do. I am an older man, so I must do my best to keep warm."

"How many years are you, Bor?"

He chuckled. "I don't know if I can answer that, to be honest. I believe I've lost count."

"How many years have you been searching for orphans? And where do you go?" Loki interjected. He wanted more information from the man.

"Mostly I travel to the royal burghs—Edinburgh and Ayr are the cities where I find the most orphans, though I have also traveled to Glasgow on occasion. Some are not orphans at all, but were dropped at the markets in Edinburgh because their parents had too many mouths to feed. They leave the eldest ones, or the ones who can help them the least.

"I can hold up to fifteen orphans. Bestla is my dear wife. There are other women who assist her with the others, especially when I leave on my journeys. The older children must learn to help, too. Basically, when I lose a few, I search for more. They grow up and move on."

Kenzie looked more confused than ever. "So did you come to me in my dreams? I do not understand any of it," he huffed out.

Loki knew exactly how his son felt. Why had the man told them to hurry? Why would he have come to the two of them at all?

"Kenzie, people who have dreams like that often have them because they are confused. Are you confused about something?"

Kenzie glanced at Loki again, and Loki nodded. It was time for him to tell all. "I loved my mama and papa verra much, but they died from the fever." His eyes misted so he swiped at them roughly. "Then I lived behind the inn and I was always cold and hungry. Now I have a new mama and papa."

"Why would you leave your new clan at this time of the year? The winter solstice is almost upon us. Don't you all celebrate with mid-winter feasts and merriment?"

"Aye, and I did not wish to come because Mama's about to have a new babe, and I'm worried I'll miss Aunt Maddie's giant banquet of food, and Grandpapa and Grandmama are at our keep and I love them. But is it wrong to love them and my true parents and Loki and Bella all together? Would my sire be angry with me if he knew I'd traveled to live with another?" He wiped a hand over his forehead as if exhausted by all the thoughts running through his head. "The man in furs came to me and he, nay, *you* told me to bring my papa to Ayr, but I don't understand why, and Grandmama said something that confuses me even more."

"What did she tell you?"

"She said that the more love you give, the more you will receive."

"And you don't understand that?"

"Nay. How do you receive love? They all give to me—food and clothes and hugs and a slinger and friends—and I don't know how to give love back. What if they change their mind and want me to go away..." The tears erupted in full at his last comment.

"That will never happen," Loki said firmly. "We all love you, Kenzie. We would never let you leave unless you were grown and wished to go somewhere else. Then it would be your choice."

"Kenzie, I think you should visit my cottage," Bor said. "Come and see the bairns I have living with me. Mayhap it will answer some questions you have."

"May we go, Papa? I want to see the lad who lived in our spot."

"Where is your cottage, Bor?"

"Closer to Edinburgh. If we leave early, we shall be there by high sun."

⟡

In the middle of the night. Loki bolted up from his bed, wondering where he was. Once he recalled their plight, he rubbed his eyes to get the sleep from them.

The man in the furs had returned in his dream *again*, but this time his hood had hidden his entire face.

"Why do you not ask the man?" the hooded figure asked. "Just come out and ask him what you wish to know."

Loki shook his head, refusing to ask any questions. Kenzie was managing to get many of their answers, so there was no need for him to admit that he, too, was experiencing the dreams.

In response, the man said, "But Kenzie does not know the answers you seek, does he? You are the only one who knows what tears at your insides. Ask the question."

The man of furs was correct again. If he wished to be free of what haunted him, he needed to be open about it. His mother had named him Lucas, so who had given him the name of Loki?

It was a simple question, and yet his soul would not rest until he found the answer.

☾

Fergus found his way back to the inn. He'd left again in the middle of the night, his soul unsettled. He brushed his fingers through the red beard he'd grown to warm his face for winter, then did his best to straighten his long locks. The ends had begun to curl. Mayhap he should have cut it, but it would keep his neck warm through the cold Highland winter. He had been born with the same coloring as his only brother Finlay, but Finlay's had darkened while his remained a strong red. He was a bit shorter than his brother, though he'd spent much time working in the lists to build up his strength. His shoulders had broadened from the frequent swordplay.

Ever since Finlay had become Jamie's second, Fergus had felt a bit lost. For a time, he and Finlay had both hoped to be Loki's second, competing for the revered position, but their mother's illness had called them home.

As far as Fergus was aware, no one had yet been assigned that coveted position. Though he was loath to leave his father and brother, he could not get much closer to Clan Grant than Castle Curanta. After they returned from their trip, mayhap he'd ask Loki for the title he still wanted.

He had two goals now. One was to impress Loki, and the second was to find the lass of his dreams. She was close—he could feel it. But where? He'd spent the night searching all of Ayr, asking everyone he encountered if they'd ever seen a lass who looked like the one he desperately sought.

Naught. Nothing. No one.

Where the hell would he find her?

CHAPTER SIX

THEY ARRIVED AT BOR'S COTTAGE the middle of the day, just as he'd suggested. As soon as he opened the door, a flurry of wee feet chased toward him, all pushing forward to hug Father Bor, as they called him. There were two older women with the bairns, and while one stood at the hearth, stirring a pot filled with some kind of stew, the other rushed to the door to greet the latest member of the Bor family.

"Bestla, this is Amice or Ami as I call her," Bor said, ushering the girl forward. "She's quite fond of Kenzie here, but she's in desperate need of a warm bath." He proceeded to introduce their guests and then handed the lass over to Bestla's capable hands. The wee bairn held her arms out to Kenzie, though she never made a sound.

"Do you think 'tis possible she cannot hear? I met someone like that once," Kenzie said. "He could not hear or speak."

Bor tipped his head back and forth and said, "Mayhap 'tis possible. I once knew a couple who gave their child away because he could not speak."

Bestla gasped, giving Bor a stern look as she handed Ami off to Kenzie. "For shame. Imagine doing such a thing to an innocent bairn." Shaking her head and clucking her tongue, the woman continued about her task, finding a small tub out in the back and ordering the older boys to heat water and fill it when ready. All the while, Ami kept a strong grip on Kenzie, her wide eyes taking in the bustle of activity around her.

Bor waved for Loki and the others to follow him, but Fergus said, "I'll see the horses settled, check the area with the guards."

Loki nodded, wondering why Fergus had been acting so odd of late though he had a suspicion it had to do with a lass, but the thought faded quickly. His focus was on getting answers. Bor led them through the large cottage, indicating the small bed chamber he shared with Bestla. He then walked into the next chamber, twice the size of his and littered with small pallets, blankets, and plaids everywhere. "This is where all the bairns sleep."

"Where do you get the coin to feed so many wee ones, Bor?" Loki asked. "I'm sure you have a garden of your own, but you have no hunters amongst you, have you?"

"Nay, no hunters, but I have much support. Many people recognize my work as necessary and are happy to share what they have. I bring sacks of grain and apples home, skeins of wool, and the women in the area are always willing to help me. You need not worry about us. We are indeed blessed."

Kenzie hopped from one foot to the other, his usual way of indicating he had a question to ask.

"What is it, Kenzie?" Bor asked with a warm smile.

"The lad from behind the inn. Which one is he?"

Father Bor nodded. "I'll find him for you, lad." He moved back into the main chamber, warmed by the big hearth on the far wall. Loki followed him out, hoping the lad would be willing to talk with his son. He recalled exactly how hardened one could become from living in such harsh conditions.

"Bestla," Bor said, "the lad from behind the inn? The sickly one. Where is he?" His gaze scanned the crew of young faces, all staring up at him.

Loki noticed one difference between these ones and the children living with Clan Grant—the lack of laughter. He did see an occasional smile, saw some lassies huddled near the hearth singing to each other, but it was a most sad arrangement. While he didn't doubt Bor's work brought the bairns to a better place, he still had to wonder about their happiness. He moved to the door off the back and peeked out, noticing several older lads chopping wood, or practicing with a bow and arrow.

Hellfire, he'd have to shoot a boar before he left. The children were all too thin.

"Papa!"

Kenzie's squeal brought him back inside just in time for him to catch the lad as he sailed through the air at him. The lad clung to him like a limpet, sobbing. Loki glanced at Bor, hoping for an explanation of the lad's sudden change in temperament.

"The lad from the inn passed on," Bor said, his tone much less cheerful. "I thought perhaps he was too sickly to bring home, but it was worth an attempt."

Kenzie's tears abated for a short moment. "At least he was warm when he passed on. I thought surely I'd die in the cold some days." He clutched his father's tunic and whispered, "Promise me you'll not send me back. Please, Papa? Please?"

Loki said, "I know not where you get such a foolish idea, but we'll not be giving you away to anyone. Ever. We'd not allow you to leave, so stop that foolish thinking or you'll make me daft from worrying about you."

"Papa, should we not take them all home with us?"

Bor came up behind him. "And leave me alone? You'll not do that to me. Now I understand their sadness. We've lost a dear lad, though we only knew him for a short time. I think we must head to Edinburgh's market to get something special to cheer the bairns. I'd be honored to have you travel with me, Kenzie."

Kenzie dropped to the floor and wiped his tears. "Aye, I'd like to go, Papa. May we go?"

"Aye, since we are not far. We'll look for a gift for your mama, Kenzie."

Just then, a wee form found her way to Kenzie, tugging on his plaid. Ami had apparently become fond of him. She was nearly unrecognizable now that her hair had been washed and her skin was scrubbed free of the dirt. Her red hair glowed in the light of the fire, and her innocent green eyes stared up at Kenzie as she held her wee hands up to him. The lad fell to the floor and she settled on his lap and plopped her thumb back in her mouth.

"You've found a new friend, lad," Father Bor chuckled. "Edinburgh is less than two hours from here. We could leave on the morrow."

"If it would please you, I'd like to leave today,"

Loki said. "My wife is carrying and her time is nigh. I would like to be back before then."

"We could go today, could we not, Father Bor?"

"Aye. How about in another hour? We'll have a drink of ale, settle the bairns, and then leave. Will that suit you, Loki?"

Loki nodded, an odd feeling coursing through him—the anticipation that something important was about to happen, or could now be happening, at home. He couldn't explain it, but there was no denying it either. A tug of longing pulled at him. He didn't like to spend time away from his Bella.

They found their way to the large trestle table in the middle of the room and enjoyed a short repast. There was still no sign of Fergus, so he decided to go outside to seek him out.

When he found him, he was not tending to the horses at all, but questioning some of the young lads behind the cottage. To Loki's surprise, Bor had followed him out of the cottage.

"Fergus, we're headed to Edinburgh to pick up some supplies. Coming along, aye?"

Fergus spun around, but his gaze went to Bor. "Is there any chance you've seen a beautiful young woman with dark, wavy hair, traveling with a wee lass? They would have arrived in the area within the last moon. She was living at Lochluin Abbey, but she left to take her own cottage."

Bor glanced from Loki to Fergus, the smile disappearing from his face. "What of the lass? Do you know her?"

"Aye," Fergus said, his eyes growing wide with excitement. It was obvious from his expression he hadn't expected an affirmative answer. "I met her at the abbey. I'd like to see her again."

"I doubt she's any more interested in you than she would be in any man."

"Listen, I know this sounds odd, but I'd like to see if we would suit. I'm asking for the opportunity to chat with her, mayhap court her. If she sends me away, I'll accept it."

Bor thought for a moment before he nodded. "She's in the cottage at the end of the ravine."

"Many thanks, Bor," Fergus replied, already moving in that direction. "I'll be here when you return, Loki. You don't need me to come along, do you?"

Loki shook his head, baffled by the exchange. Who could Fergus be seeking? How had he known she would be here? "I'll take six guards, leave the others with you," he said. "We shall return soon." When they left an hour later, a strange feeling was still seeping through Loki's pores, though he couldn't explain it to anyone.

C

Fergus was secretly glad Loki had left for Edinburgh. This meant he would have a day or two to seek out Davina's favor.

He feared he had become infatuated with her, but each time he relived their encounter in his mind, he knew it was more than that. There was something special about her, something special about their meeting. He let his mind drift back to it as he made his way to her cabin.

It was the day after the great battle with the Buchans, and all of the warriors were gathered on Cameron land. Fergus had gotten up early to do his duty as a protector for Clan Grant, in part because of the coming festivities. His baby brother Finlay was about to marry Alex Grant's eldest daughter. Who would have guessed? He was thrilled for both of them and determined to do his part to make certain none of the stragglers who'd survived the battle on Buchan land would follow them here.

Jake Grant, one of the two lairds of Clan Grant, had sent a group of warriors, including Fergus and others from Clan Grant, Clan Ramsay, and Clan Cameron, to the perimeter of Cameron land to patrol for anyone who didn't belong. The wedding would be held in haste partly to prevent word from traveling through the land. The vagabonds would be tempted by the prospect of a wedding.

Kyla Grant, the bride-to-be, didn't know that, but no one would tell her until later.

"Split up," Cailean MacAdam of Clan Ramsay yelled. "I want this done quickly. We've seen no evidence of any marauders."

Fergus was directed toward Lochluin Abbey. He didn't hesitate and headed in the direction of the abbey.

An hour later, he'd found nothing and was about to head back when a scream rent the air, sending him crashing through the bushes and into the nearby forest where the sound had originated.

The sight he'd come upon in the woods would always haunt him. A lass stood between two filthy men, who were laughing and tossing her back and forth between them in fun, groping her wherever they wished.

Fergus unsheathed his sword. "Step back from the lass, or I'll cut your hands off."

Both men spun around in surprised. "Aye, you'd

like a piece of this sweet one? Well, you'll have to wait your turn. She's mine first. I found her."

The lass spun around, kicking and scratching, fighting harder than anyone he'd ever seen, but there were two of them, tugging on her still, and she was overpowered.

Fergus had two choices. He could go for help, or he could risk taking both of them on at once.

His question was answered as soon as he pulled his gaze from the two bastards and caught hers. She was beautiful and scared for her life. He'd never seen that kind of expression up close. One of her attackers then made a fatal mistake.

He slapped her. She spat on the fool, something that surprised and pleased Fergus, but it wasn't nearly enough. His sire had taught him never to raise his hand to a woman—and never to allow anyone else to do so either. The fury that built inside him knew no bounds, so he jumped off his horse and went for the bastard.

The lass's attacker released her for a moment and reached for his sword. As soon as the man unsheathed his weapon, Fergus whipped his sword around in a power move across his body and sliced into the man's side, forcing him to drop the weapon.

The second man ran straight at him while the lass screamed. He repositioned and brought the flat of his sword against the man's arm, forcing him to drop his weapon mid-air. He then plunged the point of his sword straight into his belly, killing him instantly.

Fergus removed his sword, cleaning it on the bastard's clothes. He glanced sideways just in time to catch the lass running straight into the forest, the worst direction possible. He shouted, "Nay, there could be more."

She didn't listen, instead running as if she were still being chased.

"I'll not hurt you. I'll take you where you wish to go."

She ignored him. Blast it, but he'd have to chase her. His mother's voice flashed through is mind. When he was younger, and a wee lassie had fallen over a big boulder, his momma had said, "Help her, Fergus. You're bigger than she is."

"Stop. I'll help you! But you're headed back into danger." She continued to ignore him and then surprised him when she stopped short, bent over, and lifted a bairn out of a spot covered with moss. When he reached her, he stared in shock at the bairn, still sound asleep in her mother's arms.

The lass spun around and stared at him. "You touch me or this bairn, and I'll do all I can to hurt you."

The fury and pain in her eyes told him she meant every word. "I believe you. I saw you fight two men by yourself, driven by something. Now I know what." He nodded toward the sleeping babe. "To insult me by thinking I'd hurt a woman is one thing, but a wee bairn? Never." He took a deep breath, doing his best to stop his panting. "Where are you going?"

She swiped a lone tear from her cheek. "We're headed to the abbey. If you'd be so kind, I'd appreciate the escort, but if you're looking for favors in return, kiss my arse."

He couldn't help but laugh. She stared at him wide-eyed in shock.

"Forgive me," he said quickly. "I've never heard that word from a lass's lips before. Had many *lads* tell me to kiss their arse, but this is a first." To his surprise she giggled, a sound that was sweet as any he'd ever heard. "My name is Fergus."

"You belong to Clan Grant," she said, perusing his plaid. There was a raw edge to the words.

"Aye. You don't approve of Clan Grant?"

"I'm Davina Buchan. Your clan just killed my sire."

"My apologies for your loss, but..."

She tossed her hair as she spun her head to the side, staring off into the trees. "Aye, I know of all the trouble he's caused. You need not tell me. Had he not hired de La Porte and imprisoned Kyla Grant, things could have turned out verra differently. I was in the thick of the entire episode." Her bairn fussed a wee bit, and Davina leaned down to kiss her head.

Fergus removed his glove and reached over, running his hand over the bairn's bare head, rubbing the wee one in a calming motion that soothed her cries, though he was as surprised as Davina was about his success. "Your daughter?"

"Aye, my beautiful daughter, Raina."

"A wonderful motivation to kick and scratch. I applaud your strength. Now, may I escort you to the abbey?"

She glanced up at him and said, "Aye. And my thanks for your assistance with those fools."

He took in her situation. Despite her messy hair and muddied clothing, she was still an incomparable beauty with her raven dark hair and dark eyes. "You must take care to guard yourself against attackers. A beautiful noblewoman is a rare thing to find in the forest alone."

"I needed to protect myself from my sire's second. 'Tis the reason I am on the run. I did not wish to see him after the battle."

Fergus cleared his throat, thinking about how best to give her the news, but decided to be direct. "Your sire's second did not survive. My brother killed him in battle."

"That pleases me. I'd still like to go to the abbey, see if the nuns will accept me."

They started walking back toward his horse, and Fergus tried to bar her sight of the worst of the gore. When they reached his horse, he turned to face her, looking into her eyes, and asked, "May I assist you?" Once she nodded her permission, he lifted her onto his horse, her child snugly in her arms, and climbed up behind her once he'd adjusted his sword. They didn't speak until he dismounted in front of the abbey. He reached for her, but then paused and asked that same question again. "May I assist you?"

She nodded, though he could see the uneasiness in her eyes, something that struck him as incredibly sad. He wished to wash that fear away from her forever.

Once he lifted her down, she turned to him, snuggling her daughter close to her, then nodded to him. "My thanks, Fergus, for being honorable enough to ask for my permission to touch me— and for not taking advantage of that permission to grope me elsewhere. I thank you for your escort."

Davina had haunted Fergus ever since.

He'd seen her outside the abbey a few days later, and she'd waved to him, but that had been their only other encounter. How he would like to talk with her, spend time with her…

If nothing else, he wished to help her. Kyla Grant had explained everything the woman had been forced to deal with in her short life. The lass had been promised to Simon de La Porte, and her child's father was the most renowned villain in the land of the Scots in the last decade.

Fergus had gone back to the abbey not long after, hoping to properly speak with Davina and, if all went well, express his intention to court her, but she was already gone. His other trips to Buchan and Cameron land had been spent searching for her. Now, against the odds, he'd found her.

He often felt as though his dear mother watched him from above, and something told him she had brought him here—to this place where he could finally speak with her and make his case.

After Loki left, Fergus headed toward the ravine. Would she accept his courtship?

His hands turned clammy despite the cold weather, and his heart pounded hard enough to climb up his throat. Still, he persevered and knocked on the door.

When it opened, he looked straight into the eyes of one of the most beautiful women in all the Highlands. He cleared his throat and plunged forward.

"Greetings, Davina."

CHAPTER SEVEN

DAVINA BUCHAN STARED AT THE red-headed man in the door of her small cottage. He looked vaguely familiar, and his plaid declared him a Grant. This man was much larger than Ranulf, and something about him struck her. It took her a moment to realize what it was.

This was the man who'd saved her when she'd run to the abbey. He'd killed two men in her defense and then escorted her to her temporary home at the abbey. The biggest surprise was that he hadn't tried anything inappropriate, something quite rare. Her sire should have protected her from such gropings, but once she turned ten and six, he'd declared it her duty to the clan to please important men.

Fergus had also been kind to Raina, his touch gentle and soothing. Now, as he stood on her doorstep staring at her, she noticed something new about him. Something she hadn't noticed at the abbey.

His eyes.

His eyes were the oddest shade of green with blue flecks in them. The day in the forest had been overcast, so she'd not noticed them. They were beautiful, and the most beautiful part about them was how they reached for her soul, pulling her toward him slowly. They so mesmerized her that she realized she'd been walking toward him without realizing it. Reflexively, she took a step back, hugging her sleeping daughter closer to her chest.

"Nay, please don't walk away."

She had no idea what to say to this man, or why he'd come looking for her. She'd vowed never to have anything to do with another man again. Her own father had offered her up like a decadent sweet to different men of his choosing. She'd only loved one of them, but Ranulf MacNiven, father to her dear daughter, had gone mad. After the battle at her father's keep, she'd found her way to Lochluin Abbey and hidden there for a short time. She'd met Bor there, and he offered her this cottage, no exchanges needed, other than to assist Bestla if she requested it.

"I've been searching for you everywhere, Davina. I don't know if you recall our brief encounter in the woods outside Lochluin Abbey, but ever since then, I've hoped to talk with you again and to see how you and your daughter have fared. Please don't shut me out. Give me a chance."

"A chance for what?" If he even thought to mention the word coupling, she'd slice his manhood off for sure.

"A chance to get to know you better. I seek the chance to earn your trust. I…I know what your father expected of you, so I cannot imagine how difficult your life has been. Mayhap we would suit. I could offer you a better life than your sire gave you."

Her gasp couldn't be controlled. How her own

father had treated her was one of the most shameful parts of her life, and this man clearly knew the truth.

"Do not be embarrassed. 'Tis not your fault. Your sire bears the shame of your treatment, not you."

"My sire is dead, as is my daughter's sire, Ranulf." The death of her father caused her no pain, but the loss of Ranulf still hurt, though his true soul had died long before the blood stopped flowing through his heart. In the end, he'd been consumed by greed and ambition.

She'd sworn off missing both of them many moons ago. Ranulf had given her this babe in her arms, and that was enough.

Nay, she did not need a man in her life to use her, to hurt her, to suck the life from her again.

As if reading her thoughts, Fergus said, "I would never hurt you or raise a hand to you. My sire raised me to treat women kindly. On the honor of my mother's dear life, which was lost a short time ago, I swear never to physically hurt you. I cannot truthfully say I'd never hurt your feelings, for it may happen unwittingly, but I'd like to try."

"And what could you possibly do for me? I don't need a lover." The tears that slid down her cheek couldn't be stopped.

"One thing. Give me the chance to do one nice thing for you, and I'll take my leave if you still wish it."

"What?" Her steely reserve suddenly softened, if only a touch. No matter how hard she fought, loneliness still crept in to cause an ache in her heart on occasion. She couldn't help but remember the connection Kyla and Finlay had shared...

how deeply they loved each other. Sometimes she wished she could have that for herself, but she feared it was not meant to be.

"I'd wipe the tears from your cheeks if you'd allow me that simple pleasure."

She set her sleeping daughter down in the cradle. When she stood up again, she nodded to him. "You have less than a minute."

He strode over to her and reached for her cheek, but her instincts took over and she flinched.

"Nay, you never need to fear my touch," he whispered. "Please?"

She leaned toward him again and his hand came up to settle on her cheek, his thumb wiping the tear before it fell. It was the softest caress she'd ever felt in her life. She recalled their short encounter. This was the man who'd asked before touching her, who hadn't taken advantage of her when she sat ahorse in front of him. He'd been polite and kind, expecting nothing in return.

Their chance meeting had given her hope when she needed it most.

Her stalwart reserve crumbled and she fell forward, her head landing on his shoulder. He wrapped his arms around her and she sobbed. She cried uncontrollably for almost half an hour and the most surprising thing happened.

Fergus held her the entire time.

☾

Once Loki and the others arrived in Edinburgh, they left their horses at the stables in town so they could walk to the marketplace. Kenzie's questions began as soon as they started down the path.

"What are you here to buy, Father Bor? Do you come here often, Father Bor? Who is your favorite vendor?"

Bor chuckled before he replied, "One question at a time, lad. I come here a few times a year for supplies we may need. I'm always searching for wee lost souls, but I don't always find them. This time of year, I come for gifts."

"Gifts?"

"Gifts for the wee ones. The winter solstice is almost upon us, is it not? Do you exchange gifts in your home?"

Kenzie glanced up at his sire. "Nay. Do you?"

"I do. I bring the wee ones gifts each year. It helps them forget their losses, if only for a little while. They look forward to it every year, and sometimes their excitement starts a full moon before the solstice is upon us."

Loki asked, "Where were you born, Bor? Is this something you did at home? Are your parents from a faraway land? I've not heard of this sort of celebration before, only the English festivities. My aunt celebrates Christmas like they do."

"I'm not sure I can answer that question. I've spent time with many different people of varied backgrounds. The Norse love their solstice, and they make merry every year, though they celebrate for at least a fortnight, sometimes more. The English also love to adorn their homes with greens and decorations at this time of year."

"Aye, my aunt Maddie does the same!" Kenzie piped up. "You should see her hall. 'Tis beautiful and smells so sweet. She has pines and greens and red ribbons everywhere. They have a festive table full of every meat pie and sweet tart possible."

Loki grinned at him, remembering the lad's comment about not knowing how to repay those he loved.

Bor asked, "So if you love that gift she gives you every year, then why not find a gift for her and bring it to her?" he asked. "In fact, Aunt Maddie sounds just like the person to help you understand the gifts your grandmama told you about. Why do you think she holds the feast every year?"

"For Uncle Alex. He's big and eats more than anyone."

"Is he the only one, do you think?" Loki asked.

Bor smirked. "Even I can answer that one, Kenzie. And I do not live with you. Are there other people in her family?"

The confused expression on Kenzie's face indicated he didn't follow their meaning.

Loki looked at him with a small smirk. "To start, Jake, Jamie, Kyla, Elizabeth, and Maeve. Is the feast not for them, too?"

"Och, and Aline and Gracie and Finlay," Kenzie added, a bit of understanding showing on his face.

"Who are they?" Father Bor asked.

"Uncle Alex and Aunt Maddie's children and their spouses," Loki replied. "Can you not think of anyone else?"

Kenzie's brow furrowed again. "Aline's other sister?"

"Aye, and what about you?"

He laughed in delight. "'Tis true. Aunt Maddie loves to cook for us, too."

"Ashlyn?"

"Aye."

"Robbie and Grandpapa?" Loki asked.

"Aye."

"Caralyn and Grandmama?" Loki asked.

"Aye."

Father Bor said, "Are you understanding their meaning yet, lad?"

"Nay." He paused for a moment, his forehead scrunched with thought, and said, "Aunt Maddie cooks for everyone, I suppose. I mean, she does not do all the cooking because the Grants have the best cook of all, but she helps and plans the meals. But is that not what she's supposed to do? My first mama cooked when Papa worked the land. 'Twas what they were supposed to do."

"Who is the most revered on Grant land?"

Kenzie gasped. "Aunt Maddie!"

"So? What does that make you think? And remember what Grandmama told you," Bor said.

"That everyone loves Maddie because of all she does at the winter solstice?"

"And all year long," Loki added. "She does it out of love. Why do you think your papa worked the land and your mother cooked?"

His eyes lit up. "Because they loved me?"

Loki nodded. "And each other."

Bor said, "Maddie should get gifts and affection from everyone because she does things for everyone, Kenzie. Do you see?"

"Because she gives so much, everyone loves her more?" Kenzie asked, a perplexed expression on his face.

"Exactly."

"Then I know what I must do. Papa, I must buy a gift for everyone."

Loki and Bor exchanged knowing glances. "Great idea. And why?"

"So they won't give me away."

Loki groaned.

"Is that not right, Papa? Am I wrong again?"

"Nay, we'll find something for whomever you like." He tipped his head toward Bor. "And hope he'll understand it when he gets home."

"He's a smart lad. He'll decipher our meaning. I think he's still a wee bit nervous about being left behind." Bor chuckled and moved over to the first stall full of chestnuts. "Here's something I love to bring to the wee ones. The older ones help the younger ones dig the sweet meat out of the shells."

"Uncle Brodie and Uncle Robbie love those," Loki said. "We better get a dozen or so."

They exchanged coin for the chestnuts and moved down to the next stall full of woolen goods. "Papa," Kenzie said, looking at him with wide eyes, "I wish to get Mama a warm pair of stockings. Verra thick ones. She says her feet are often cold. Remember how she likes to sit by the fire on cold nights?"

"I think 'tis a great idea. Which ones would you like?"

Their group traveled from stall to stall, Kenzie enjoying selecting presents for each person he could think of. By the time they were ready to leave, they had two sacks full of gifts. They had collected food items, ribbons, a couple of daggers, special fragrant oils for Grandmama, dried flowers, and some special spices and herbs, but Loki's favorite gift by far was the tapestry Kenzie had found.

"Does it not look just like Grant Castle, Papa?

Uncle Alex and Aunt Maddie will love it."

"I couldn't agree more."

It took them several hours to move through the conglomeration of vendors, and at the end of the evening, they found an inn where they could seek some repast and spend the night.

Loki found a chamber with two beds and Bor found his own accommodation. They enjoyed a thick mutton stew before they settled in for the night.

In the middle of the night, Loki awakened to a small face directly in front of his. "Papa, are you awake?"

"Yes, I am now." He couldn't wait until something put a stop to these endless dreams.

"I think we should take her home."

"What?"

"Ami, Amice. I think we should take her home with us. She could be a friend to the new bairn if it's a lassie. She truly favors me, and I think she'll be upset when we leave. I...I'm worried something will happen to her, Papa."

"I'll consider it. Can we decide on the morrow, Kenzie?" Sleep, he just needed some sleep. Everything would be clearer in the morning.

Kenzie lowered a voice to a deep whisper. "Papa, Father Bor is verra nice, but he's not a mama and Bestla's too busy. Ami needs a mama like mine. You know Grandmama will help Mama take care of her. Please?"

Loki sighed. "We'll talk in the morn. Go to sleep."

In truth, the same thought had occurred to him. He hoped Bella would welcome Ami into their home.

CHAPTER EIGHT

𝒞

FERGUS INHALED DAVINA'S SWEET AROMA as he held her. Her head was tucked neatly under his chin, and her curves fit him just right. How could he make her believe that they deserved a chance at happiness? How could he help her overcome the wounds of the past?

He'd asked Jake Grant about his wife Aline, who'd been abused by a bastard. Not wanting to reveal his intentions, he'd simply made a comment about how difficult it must have been to handle such a situation.

Jake, not usually a talkative man, had given him only one word—slowly.

So he vowed to take the same approach. He'd hold her forever if she wished for it.

She shoved at his chest and stepped back. "Leave me be. Forgive my weak moment, but I don't need a man in my life."

"I will do as you wish." He stepped back and put his hands behind his back in a totally non-threatening stance. "Is there anything I can do to help you?"

"Nay. Go. I allowed you your one request." She glanced up at him, but wouldn't meet his eyes. "I'll thank you for holding me and allowing me my moment of weakness."

"Forgive me for disagreeing, but crying is not a weakness. You have every right to feel emotional. I expected to still find you at Lochluin Abbey. Why did you leave?"

"I didn't exactly have the same view of life as the nuns. My entire existence is for my daughter, and I will do anything for her. I was grateful they took us in when Raina and I needed it most, but I could not stay there forever." Her gaze drifted away from him.

He wondered what her thoughts were. What did she think of her living conditions? She lived in a small cottage with a dirt floor, covered with old rushes, a musty smell permeating everything. It was uncluttered, illustrating that she had few belongings. An old kettle hung over the hearth with something simmering inside, but there was little aroma to tempt him. The wood bin next to the hearth was empty.

The cottage had one table with two chairs, a small bed in the corner with a few furs and a threadbare plaid. The only other item was the cradle, where her daughter still slept under a fox fur. Davina wore a shabby silk dress, one that had probably been regal before it was stained and wrinkled by her hard life.

She was the only daughter of the once-mighty Glenn of Buchan. The man's ambition had twisted his mind and ruined his family, and now his only daughter wore rags and her glossy hair was plaited away from her face.

She was still as beautiful as ever to Fergus.

"Please just go." She didn't look at him as she

said it. Rather, the words were whispered at the far wall.

Not knowing what else to do, he bowed to her and took his leave. She never said another word, allowing him to walk out of her life.

His worst fear had just happened. He had finally found her, but he'd failed to move her. He'd failed to persuade her that they could live a good life together, that they should be given a chance for happiness. Once outside the cottage, he thought of the empty bin by the hearth. True, Bor probably would send some lads down to cut wood for her, but then he was perfectly capable, wasn't he?

Would she turn him away for cutting wood?

He decided to do it anyway. He walked to the rear of the cabin, found an axe, and searched for the best tree to drop.

&

Davina let a breath out as soon as the door closed. Fergus MacNicol didn't realize how much she wished for him to stay. In her dreams, a man loved her, cherished her, and adored her daughter. After meeting Fergus at the abbey, her knight had come to her with red hair. He would be a wonderful father, and a protector. He'd keep the men with wandering hands and expectant gazes away from her. He'd love her for who she was and not for the size of her breasts and what lay between her legs.

Ranulf had taught her what love could be, how special it could be to be held by a man, to feel worshipped, to love another through your body.

To *feel*.

She wanted that again, but with a man who would

not turn daft over revenge and greed. She wanted a simple life, a safe haven to raise her daughter away from cruelty and leering gazes.

Did such a place exist?

She'd let Fergus go, fearful he would be like nearly every other man she'd ever met, but the dreams stayed with her…they argued that she'd been wrong to send him away. That this was a mistake she would not stop regretting. A loud sound caught her attention. After glancing to be sure Raina still slept, she moved to the window in the back of the house and pulled the fur back to see what had made the noise. If it was a wild animal, perhaps her screams would reach Fergus's ears before he was too far away.

She peeked out of the window, shocked to see Fergus had found an axe and felled a tree.

The man was a beast. He'd stripped down to his tunic and plaid, though how he could withstand the cold, she knew not. She watched him lift the axe over his head and bring it down on the tree in one smooth move, the muscles in his back rippling with every effort and movement he made. The lines of his body could be seen through his tunic. Och, how she wished to reach out and remove his tunic so she could watch him in his glory— all strength and brawn, the cords in his neck even standing out with each swing of the tool.

From where she stood, she could see the fine sheen of sweat bead up and trickle down the side of his face. An unexpected thought surfaced in her head. She could stop it from dripping onto his tunic by catching it with her tongue.

A small moan escaped her lips, and somehow he

heard her. Spinning around, he lifted the axe over his head as if to strike an enemy down, only to drop it to the ground upon seeing her.

He stared at her, but she couldn't move. A paralyzing moment stretched between the two of them until she dropped the fur and reached for the back door, flinging it open. He reached her in two steps, the heat of his gaze and his body drawing her to him until her hands cupped his face and she whispered, "Love me."

He took her in his arms and kissed her, a searing kiss that woke her entire body up, rousing a rippling need that had long since died. Passion coursed through her with such persuasive power that she gave in, allowing it to take over her thoughts. She ran her hands over his muscular body, dropped his plaid to the floor and tugged at his tunic until he removed it and flung it off to the side. He lifted her and carried her to the bed, standing her up long enough to remove her gown and chemise before lowering her to the bed and covering her with his body.

His hands moved to her breasts as he moaned, lifting one mound to take it into his mouth, suckling her nipple until she cried out. He raked his teeth across the sensitive peak and she thought she'd climax right then, but he played with her a bit longer, his hand settling between her legs until he found her slick entrance.

She touched him everywhere she could, reveling in the hardness of his body, finally reaching for his cock and settling it between her legs.

"Now," she gasped. He entered her swiftly, plunging into her again and again, pausing just once.

"I knew we would be wonderful together. I knew it." He kissed a trail up her neck before he took her lips in his, ravaging her with his tongue.

He kept the rhythm up, and she nudged his hip just a bit to get him exactly where she wanted him. His response was to reach down and caress her nub, causing her to cry out as she climaxed, her legs spreading wide with a need she still didn't understand but didn't fight.

He clutched her hips and came with a roar, her name on his lips moments later as he did his best to calm his panting.

"I love you, Davina," he declared as he nuzzled her neck, his breath still hitching. He kissed her forehead and whispered, "I know we haven't known each other long, but I know you're the only woman for me. I promise to love you and protect you forever. Please give us a chance."

Her hands still clutched his shoulders as she rocked him just a bit more, locking him inside her woman's place, not wanting their moment to end.

Then she gazed up at him and said, "I'll try." Her fingers caressed his bottom lip, then fingered his beard.

He nodded and said, "That's all I ask."

With a coldness that even surprised herself, she whispered, "Fair warning to you. If you ever hit me or my daughter, I'll take a blade to you in the middle of the night."

The man just never stopped. He kissed her forehead. "I would take a blade to myself before that would ever happen."

The faintest glimmer of hope lightened her heart.

CHAPTER NINE

❦

T HE NEXT MORNING, LOKI MOTIONED to Father Bor to meet him outside the chamber while Kenzie still slept. They moved down to the main room of the inn, the smell of baking bread causing his mouth to water. "A quick word, Bor."

"What is it, Loki? You still wish to head home straight away?"

"Aye, but I must speak with you before Kenzie awakens."

"What is it?"

"May we adopt Amice? Kenzie has taken a liking to the lass, and so have I."

"What? You are serious about this?" The old man rubbed the whiskers on his chin, staring intently at him. "She is quite young."

"Aye. Kenzie thinks, and do not take offense at this, but he thinks she needs a mama. His mama to be exact."

"Well, I cannot argue with the lad over that. A wee lass does need a mother, and Bestla has too many to fuss over just one. I normally don't take in bairns as young as Ami, but how could I turn her away?"

"Which church did you find her at? Do you know aught about her background?" He gave the innkeeper an order for their table, expecting Kenzie to join them shortly.

"Both parents are dead, the mother from a fever and the father shortly afterward from a fall from his horse."

"How do you know this?"

"It was the priest from your fath…" Bor stopped abruptly, changing the subject. "I just stopped at the kirk and she was there."

Loki's heart sped up. The man had almost said, "your father," Loki was sure of it. But how did he know aught about Loki's father?

The door opened and Kenzie bolted into the room. "I'm so hungry, Papa. The bread smells delicious."

"Sit down, lad. I just ordered bread and porridge for all of us." He made himself calm down, knowing he could not ask any more questions in front of the lad.

But he'd be asking Bor quite a few more questions once they arrived back at his cottage. Could Bor know something about how he had arrived in Ayr?

He vowed not to leave without answers.

※

They arrived back at Bor's place before midday. Kenzie had spent a good amount of time checking to make sure his packages did not fall to the ground. Once they stepped inside, several of the children rushed up to Bor, concerned expressions on their wee faces.

"What is it?" Bor glanced over their heads to look at Bestla, who tipped her head toward a small pallet set up not far from the hearth.

The child on the pallet struggled to get up, her eyes brightening when she saw Kenzie.

Loki noticed who it was at about the same time his son ran in that direction.

"Wee Amice has taken the fever, Bor. Naught I do calms her. She is so fretful… I fear for her terribly."

The poor lass shed tears, but little sound came from her, though a small grating sob came eventually. Kenzie picked her up and settled onto the floor next to the hearth. She leaned over his shoulder, clutching him, and fell fast asleep.

"Papa, she feels like fire," Kenzie said, his voice shaking with fear. "Her whole body burns."

Loki turned to Bestla and Bor, whose expressions were pained as they stared at the two on the floor. "We could take her to Cameron land. My aunt Jennie is one of the best healers in the land. She'll know what to do."

"How far is that?" Bestla asked.

"Mayhap a day's journey," Loki replied.

"Nay, nay, she'd never survive it. She's too weak to begin with. The child must eat to fight sickness." The poor woman kneaded her hands in front of her. "Kenzie, keep her warm."

"She's too warm already."

"There must be something we can do to help her. Kenzie, you've had the fever before," Loki said. "What do Aunt Caralyn, Aunt Jennie, and Aunt Maddie all say about the fever?"

"Drink. Aunt Jennie told Uncle Alex to drink and drink when he got the fever. He didn't want to drink and she told him she'd sit on him until he drank more." He giggled. "I thought 'twas funny. She tried to climb on him and he pushed her away, but then he drank."

"He lived?" Bestla asked.

"Aye, he's the Grant laird. He lived and he's still fighting with his sword."

"I'll get more goat's milk for her." She rushed out the door.

Kenzie called after them. "Aunt Jennie said it did not matter what he drank, but he had to keep drinking all the time."

Once she returned with a jug of milk, Loki said, "Kenzie, I must speak with Bor for a moment. Will you stay with Ami for a wee bit?"

The lad nodded and then turned back to his charge, clearly taking his job quite seriously.

"Bor, may I speak with you outside?"

"Of course." Bor led the way out the door and, instead of stopping, walked into the nearby forest, continuing on until he came to a clearing.

He turned around, giving Loki a pointed look, but Loki had no idea what the old man wanted from him. His gaze scanned the area, a small clearing surrounded by trees on all sides. Strangely enough, something pulled to him, so he walked the perimeter without any prompting from Bor, finally stopping at a tree with multiple cut marks across it. It looked as if someone had attempted to cut it down and failed. A stump was not far from it, so he sat down, staring at the tree as visions peppered his mind.

A young lad.

An axe.

Tears.

Screams.

Howling pain—the kind of pain no healer could cure, the kind that would dig at you every day.

Every day until you wanted to quit, run away, give up.

"Do you recall anything about that tree, Lucas?"

Tears flooded his eyes as it all came back to him, flitting bits and pieces of memory tugging their way out of the recesses in his mind. "You called me Lucas. You know my true sire."

Bor stood with his hands behind his back. "I did, and I do. Tell me what you remember."

Loki stared at the tree and a young lad popped in front of him, a lad angry at the world, swinging an axe at the tree over and over and over again.

The lad screamed and screamed, "I hate you, I hate you, I hate you…"

Loki stared at Bor through his tears. "Who did I hate so badly?"

"Your father, or the man you believed to be your father, and another man."

He jumped up from the tree stump as the memories returned in full. "I was angry with my father. I hated him. He wasn't truly my father, but I didn't know it then. I tried to save my mother from a beating…"

"Instead your father and his helper beat you."

"Aye. That man, Hamish, threw me in a wagon and took me away. I recalled this before…he tossed me out of the wagon expecting me to die, but I didn't."

"Nay, you were stronger than they expected you to be. You fought hard, crawled on your hands and knees until someone found you." Bor stood unmoving, his hands still behind his back.

"You. 'Twas *you* who found me." Memories of a burly, bearded man with a smile and kind eyes flooded back to him. Bor had climbed off his horse and lifted him up, giving him water and telling him he'd not die. "You saved me, brought me to Ayr."

"I did bring you to Ayr, but you'd already saved yourself. I then brought you here to live with us. Even in this place, your desire for vengeance ate at your insides. Do you remember?"

Loki's eyes widened. "I do." He paced in a circle. "I wanted to kill Hamish. Hamish and Blackett, the rat bastard who beat my mother and pretended to be my sire. Only he wasn't. He killed my mother, I'm sure of it."

"Probably. You wished to find them and make them pay. I'd hoped you would lose some of your anger if I allowed you to swing at that tree, but it never helped, until one day…"

Loki held his hand up. "Saints above, I remember. Allow me. I swung and swung, and one day, I was so angry that I told you I didn't want to be called Lucas anymore."

"Aye, you believed it tied you to Blackett, that he'd chosen the name for you."

"I hated him, so it ate at my insides…but…" So much had returned, but it still didn't all fit together. "I wanted a new name. You told me tales of the Norse gods and goddesses, and I wanted to be just like Loki."

"Aye, you wished to be the wee trickster, and you vowed you'd become one of the largest and fiercest warriors in all the land so that you could return one day to kill Blackett and Hamish. According to your true sire, you did just that."

"I did. Blackett tricked me first, but good triumphed over evil that day. I hated those rat bastards."

"Did you defeat them alone?"

Loki settled back on the stump. "Nay, only with the help of my adoptive family, Clan Grant, and our allies, the Ramsays."

"I doubt the Grants and Ramsays come together for just anyone, do they?"

He dipped his head, thinking of how fortunate he'd been to run into Brodie Grant and Fergus's sire, Nicol. "Nay, they do not. But how did you know my true sire?"

"I met him not long ago. There are not many men who have one blue eye and one green. I asked him about you, and sure enough, he was your sire. He thanked me for picking you up from the ground where I found you."

"I remember everything, but why couldn't I recall it before? I don't understand." He rested his head in his hands, trying to work this new information into the tapestry of his life.

"Because the last day you were out here swinging, you lost your balance and hit your head on a rock. It knocked you out. When you awakened, you would only answer to Loki, and you left for Ayr the next day. That's all I can tell you. As you said to Kenzie, the mind protects itself when it must."

"I had several dreams about you recently…as did my son. Why? You are the caretaker of lost children. Why would I start dreaming about you now?"

Bor grinned. "Och, I can only thank the angels

for that. I'm not sure I believe in them, but I was desperate to contact you, and I prayed for them to bring you to me."

"Why?" Loki stood up to face the old man, just now noticing how tired his eyes were, how the color of his skin had a slight yellowish cast.

Bor took a deep breath and let it out slowly, shifting his gaze from his feet back up to Loki's eyes. "Because I'll not be of this world much longer. I seek to find someone to take on my work, to keep searching for the lost souls, the weak bairns, the orphaned. Your sire told me you had your own castle, and I'd hoped you could help me."

"You want me to take all the bairns home with me now?" Loki was in shock, not sure if he could do this without first talking with his sweet Bella.

"Nay, please do not take them from me now. Bestla would be devastated. I'm not leaving yet, and you still have a challenge or two ahead of you, but I was hoping I could send a messenger to you when my time was near. And I would ask that you travel to Ayr and Edinburgh once or twice a year to find the newest lost souls, bring them to a warm home."

Loki nodded, thinking about his proposition. He knew there were many generous souls at Grant land who would gladly help him. His mother, Gracie, Kyla, Ashlyn and Magnus, Aline, and so many more. He had plenty of room in his keep, and needed to build his own people to add to the might of Clan Grant. "I'd be happy to, if you'll allow us to take Ami with us. 'Twould break Kenzie's heart to leave without her. We'll wait to leave until she's well enough to make the journey, of course."

"I can agree to that. I do not wish to lose another bairn." His sadness changed as the ends of his lips curved up ever so slightly. "So you'll come when I send a message?"

He nodded, but a voice from behind interrupted him.

"I'll help you, if you'll have me. I cannot bear to think of children living alone in the cold, hungry."

He stood, spinning around to find Fergus and Davina Buchan behind him.

"Davina? Davina Buchan?"

Fergus nodded. "We met at the abbey before Kyla's wedding. I've been searching for her ever since she left the abbey."

Davina nodded with tears in her eyes, a wee lassie attached to her hip. "I want to help the bairns. The lost souls deserve a home." She glanced at the floor as if ashamed of something. "I've been lost for a while, and I'm not proud of my past."

Bor said, "What's important is what happens now, not what happened in the past."

"That is, if you'll accept me on your land, my lord," she said to Loki. "I know I would not be welcomed by any of the Ramsays, but Kyla once told me I would be welcome on Grant land...and mayhap it would be better if I lived on your land, that is, if you'd have me."

Fergus said, "I've asked Davina to marry me, and she has accepted on the condition that we wait two moons before we marry."

Kenzie burst into the clearing. "Say aye, Papa. We're already a land of orphans. Nearly all of us have lost parents, and we belong in Castle Curanta." Kenzie hopped from one foot to the other. "'Tis why I dreamed about Father Bor, Papa. The lost souls will need a new place soon. 'Twill be *our* place."

"Aye," Loki said with a grin, patting his son on the head. "I see you all have valid points. I must discuss this with Bella and then the laird of Clan Grant, but I think 'twill work."

"I'm sorry I was eavesdropping, Papa. I know you taught me not to, but Ami fell asleep and I wanted to see if we can still take her home with us. I will help take care of her. She doesn't cry."

Bor clasped Kenzie's shoulder and said, "I send her home with you with my blessings. She is an angel in my eyes, so I want her to have a wonderful life. I hope she continues to improve."

Loki turned to Fergus. "Congratulations to you, and if you are truly interested in making Castle Curanta your home, I'd ask you to consider being my second. I would be happy to have such a hard-working warrior."

Fergus's face lit up as he glanced first at Davina and then back at Loki. "I'd be honored, my laird."

CHAPTER TEN

(

L OKI LED THE GROUP UP through the nar-
row ravine, the winds whistling through the tall
pines. He had tucked Ami under his brat against his
chest and she'd fallen asleep instantly, her wee face
almost peeking out of the top.

They'd had to wait two more days before they
dared to travel with her, but she'd steadily improved
with Kenzie's help.

The delay had forced them to miss spending the
winter solstice with the rest of the family, but it had
given him plenty of occasion to observe Davina
and Fergus as a couple. Despite the quickness of
their courtship, they definitely seemed to be a solid
couple, though Loki had sensed a touch of doubt
emerging in Davina every now and then. He'd told
her once that, in his opinion, she'd never find a
gentler warrior than Fergus MacNicol.

Davina had nodded, a tear escaping her eye, and
replied, "I believe you. He's a fine man."

Davina's daughter Raina had brightened up the
big cottage with her smiles and laughter. He knew
Kyla would be pleased to see both Davina and
Raina, but would the rest of the Grants be upset
to learn she was betrothed to one of their own?
That the young couple would be living in Castle

Curanta? Time would tell.

When they drew near Grant land, Kenzie's questions began bubbling out of him as fast as they popped into his head. "I know the winter solstice passed while we waited for Ami to get better, but do you think Aunt Maddie has saved us any food? Mayhap she saved some fruit tarts. I would share with Ami. She would love a pear tart, for certes."

They were quickly greeted by a Grant contingency led by Jamie Grant. Kenzie opened his mouth, clearly eager to ask about the tarts and the festivities, but Loki said, "I'll speak first, Kenzie. You must hold your questions."

Jamie drew up next to him on his mount. "Welcome home. Was it a productive journey for you, cousin? And is that a wee lass peeking out of your brat?"

"Aye, the lass is a long story better saved for later. Our journey was verra productive. How is Bella? And Kenzie is dying to know if we missed all the fruit tarts."

"I'm sorry, Kenzie—the feasting is done at our keep. We'll lead you on to Curanta, but Bella should be the one to tell you all that has transpired in your absence."

Loki had no idea what Jamie meant by that, or why his normally jubilant cousin looked so serious, but he decided not to read into it. They were almost home. The Grant guards surrounded them, assisting their travel through the more treacherous areas. Once they arrived at Castle Curanta, he hopped off his horse. "Forgive me," he announced to all of them, "but Jamie and Fergus will assist you from here. I must go to Bella. Jamie—" he handed

Ami over to him, "—please bring her inside but 'tis verra important that you keep her warm."

With that, he raced across his courtyard and up the steps to his hall. There were few people inside, he noticed, but all were somber, including his mother. He waved at them as soon as he was inside the door and asked, "Bella?"

"Upstairs, Loki." His mother pointed to the staircase, and he chose not to focus on the sad expression on her face. Surely it just meant that Bella hadn't delivered yet, that they were overanxious waiting for the bairn to come.

He took the steps three at a time and arrived at his chamber, opening it with a knock so as not to startle his wee wife. He stepped inside, surprised to see Gracie, Aunt Caralyn, and Aunt Maddie at Bella's bedside.

He could hear her sobs under the covers, and all he could think was the worst. Their bairn. What had happened to their bairn?

"Aunt Maddie?" he whispered.

She strode over to his side and took his hands in hers. Caralyn grasped his shoulders. "Loki," she said, "Bella lost the bairn. I'm so sorry."

Gracie came over and gave him a quick hug, mumbling some kind words, but he didn't hear them. His gaze was focused on Bella's shape under the covers.

He heard the door close behind him as the two women left, so he moved over and sat on the edge of the bed. "Bella?"

She finally popped out and threw her arms around him. "Loki, I'm so sorry, so sorry. Forgive me."

He hugged her to him, wrapping his arms around her tightly and taking in her sweet scent, which reminded him that he was home. They had lost the babe, but she was safe. "What happened? Why are you apologizing?"

She pulled back, her breath hitching between sobs. "I lost the babe. 'Twas a wee lassie, and she never took a breath."

"But why are you apologizing? 'Tis not your fault."

"Because I should have told you, but I couldn't. I just couldn't. I didn't want to believe it."

"Believe what?"

"The bairn had stopped moving in my belly." She wailed two more times before she could stop crying long enough to talk again. "I loved her so much, and I didn't wish to admit she was gone. But Caralyn had told me a sennight before you left to pay attention to the babe's movement. The babe stopped moving before you left…and she was born two days afterward. She never took a breath. I held her close and we had to bury her while you were gone. I'm so sorry. I should have told you."

"Och, sweet Belle. Do not apologize. *I'm* sorry. I wish I had been here with you. You should not have gone through it all alone."

"Oh, Loki, she was so beautiful. I wished for a way to breathe life into her, but there was no hope. She was so tiny."

Loki held Bella while she sobbed, not knowing what else to do. They'd lost a daughter. After all he'd just been through, he couldn't help but ask why this would happen now.

"Husband, Caralyn said there is a way to keep

me from carrying again. She has herbs to give me. I don't know if I can go through this again. 'Twas so painful. I hope you're not upset with me. I tried to be a good mama and eat well so she would be a big bairn, but I failed. She says we can change our minds later, but I could not handle carrying again right away. Please?"

He cupped her face. "Hush, never say such things." He kissed her tenderly, hoping to let her know how much he loved her. "Bella, you are a wonderful mother to Lucas. We have a wonderful, strong laddie, we have Kenzie, and if you wish to take the herbs, then do it. 'Twas no fault of yours. I don't believe such drivel. 'Tis God's way...and mayhap 'tis not for us to question."

A strange feeling washed over him. He didn't believe God had purposefully taken this babe from them, but mayhap He had known it would happen...mayhap that was why He'd sent the dreams to him and Kenzie. What if they hadn't gone? They would never have met Bor, never have arranged to take his place as the helpers of lost children, never have met wee Ami...

Fear gripped him as he thought about Ami downstairs. How would Bella react to the wee lass after losing her own bairn? The possibility of this loss had never occurred to him when he'd agreed to bring Ami home. Before he had time to give it any more thought, Kenzie's face peeked around the corner of the door.

"Papa, may I bring her in to meet Mama?"

Loki stared at Bella, not knowing how to tell her what they'd done. Ultimately, though, he had no choice but to speak. "Bella, the lass lost her mama.

She doesn't speak, and she had no one but an old woman and old man to care for her. Had I known you'd lost the babe, I would not have brought her to you, but she fell in love with Kenzie, and he wanted to bring her home, make her part of our family. If you don't want…"

Bella stared at him in astonishment, but then brought her finger up to his lips to quiet him. She waved to Kenzie. "You brought a bairn home with you?"

"Aye, Mama," Kenzie said. "Aunt Maddie told me about the bairn, and I'm so sorry, but Ami had no one, and she loves me, so I thought she could come home with us and be my sister. She needs a mama, and since you are the best mama in the world…" He pulled Ami in through the door. She stood next to Kenzie, gripping his leg, her thumb in her mouth as she sucked away.

Loki looked at Bella, not knowing what else to say. Her hand fell away from Loki's lips, and she waved for Kenzie to bring the lass closer. "How old is she?" Bella asked.

Kenzie stood next to the bed, Ami still gripping his arm. "Her name is Ami and she's only two summers. She's verra sweet, Mama."

Ami let go of Kenzie's leg and stood up straight, yanking her thumb out of her mouth. She looked straight at Bella and held her arms up to her.

She finally spoke her first word.

"Mama?"

CHAPTER ELEVEN

❦

BELLA LOOKED AT LOKI WITH tears in her eyes and said, "I cannot lift her, Loki. Please put her in my arms."

Loki did as she asked, settling the wee lass on the covers in front of her. The lass's green eyes looked up at her hopefully. Bella couldn't believe how perfect she was.

"Mama?" She pointed to Bella's chest. "Mama?"

"Aye, I'm your new mama, Ami. And this is your new papa and your brother Kenzie."

Ami glanced at each of them in turn, as if taking her new family's measure. "Kencie."

"Aye, Kenzie."

"You are accepting her, Bella? You're sure she will not break your heart?" Loki asked. "Please don't feel compelled to do this if you don't want to."

She shook her head, tears coming to her eyes again. "I'm sure she will break my heart someday when she marries, but not until then. She is perfect. Do you know what I wished to name our daughter? Abi. Abi and Ami. Now I understand."

Loki gave her a strange look but said, "Good, because I wish I did. If you could understand what Kenzie and I have just been through, you'd be amazed. We have much to tell you, but it can wait."

Bella cuddled the wee lassie against her. The bairn pointed to her one more time and said, "Mama," then put her thumb back in her mouth. Bella kissed the top of Ami's head as she snuggled against her.

"Did you meet the man with furs?" She'd hoped they would succeed, but it had seemed like such a stretch. It hurt her to see the people she loved tortured by the past. She'd do anything she could to protect Ami from having such troubles.

"We did," Kenzie blurted out. "He's the keeper of lost souls and he wants us to take over for him when he dies."

Loki rolled his eyes in that way she loved—his normal reaction to Kenzie's tendency to give away more information that he should. "We'll explain it all later," Loki said, "but he has the right of it. Bor is the man's name. He wants us to take over for him when he passes."

"We're the misfits," Kenzie said with a smile. "We're almost all orphans now. And Fergus brought Davina back with him. They're getting married. Lots of orphans live here."

She smiled at the two of them, something she hadn't done since they left. "I do love you two so. Thank you for believing in me enough to bring Ami home. Why don't we take her down to meet everyone in the hall? We'll never forget Abi, but I have room in my heart for another lassie, and I think you do, too, Loki."

Loki helped her out of bed and found a night rail for her to wear, then carried Ami out of the chamber and across the balcony. Bella stopped halfway to the stairs and leaned over the railing. The cluster of people gathered by the hearth waited expectantly to hear what she had to say.

"Everyone, meet our new daughter, Ami."

Ami pulled her thumb out of her mouth, pointed to Bella and said, "Mama."

The entire hall erupted in a cheer.

Nay, Bella would never forget wee Abi, but the wee lass in her husband's arms needed her. She leaned over and kissed the girl's forehead before she said, "Please, let's celebrate our new daughter, the many blessings we have, and the winter solstice."

Then she looked at Kenzie and said, "We saved it just for you, lad."

A flurry of activity took place around them, but Loki remained focused on his wife and children. He settled Bella near the hearth with Ami on her lap, piled a warm plaid atop them, and then rushed upstairs to wake Lucas from his nap. Pride filled his heart as he introduced the lad to his new sister. Lucas touched her red hair and smiled.

Fergus brought Davina over to the fireplace and introduced her to Bella. "This is my wife-to-be, Davina. Her daughter's name is Raina. I asked Loki if we could live in a hut in your bailey, but he has invited me to be his second. He said there is an open chamber upstairs we could have after we marry. I hope this is acceptable to you, my lady."

"More than acceptable. I look forward to having both of you stay in the keep. I do get lonely sometimes when Loki is traveling with the Grants."

"I'll be traveling with him, so when we go, neither of you will be alone," Fergus squeezed Davina's shoulders. "Davina may have the upstairs chamber until we wed. I'll sleep with the warriors. And the wee ones will be playmates."

Loki leaned down to kiss Bella on the cheek. "I'll be right back." He needed a moment alone after all that had happened. His mother and Aunt Maddie were tending to Bella and Ami, so he thought it a good time to leave. Stepping into the courtyard, he huddled into his clothing as he lifted his face toward the sky, surprised to see a few glittering snowflakes dusting the air. Winter was here.

A tear caught in his eye as he thought about the daughter he and Bella had lost. Abi was a most beautiful name. What would she have been like? Would she have looked like him or Bella? He strode across his land, still unable to understand the workings of the world—why one child had been given to him and another taken away. Would aught have happened differently if he had not left for Ayr? Bella seemed truly happy to accept wee Ami into their family, but had he agreed to do something that would prove to be too much for him and his clan? For his wife?

Uncle Alex came up behind him, clasping his shoulder. "My sympathies on the loss of your bairn, Loki."

He peered up at his uncle and nodded. "The loss is painful, Uncle, and I know we will always grieve her." His uncle was known for his wisdom, so he decided to ask for his opinion. "My laird, I was asked to assist someone…" He struggled for the right words, but he knew his uncle would allow him the time to form his thoughts. All he could think of was a small hut near Edinburgh full of wee ones without parents. "I met a man who provides care for orphans. He's dying and asked me if I would take over his life's mission, to seek out and care for the orphans in our land. Bring them home to Castle Curanta."

Uncle Alex thought for a moment and said, "I can't think of a better person to take over that task. What say you?"

"I agreed, but I said I would need your support and Bella's."

"Is this the man from your dreams? The one with the furs?"

"Aye. I'm having trouble believing all that transpired. If I hadn't been there, seen how closely the man matched my vision…"

"May I give a word of advice?"

"I would value it." More than anything, he needed someone to convince him he was not losing his mind.

"I don't ever say 'why me' anymore. Fate can be a wondrous facet of life if you look at it as an opportunity instead of always questioning everything. You were chosen for this calling for a reason." He clasped Loki's shoulder again. "We will support you completely when the time comes. Just tell me whatever you need."

They were interrupted by shouts from the gates. Finlay and Kyla had arrived to join the group. Once they greeted them, Alex said, "Shall we return, Loki? Are you ready? Kyla has a surprise coming to her."

Once inside, Kyla immediately rushed over to hug Davina. Loki returned to Bella's side, squeezing her hand as he took a seat on a stool nearby. The reunion put tears in both of their eyes, and it was Davina who brought Kyla over to offer her condolences to Bella and greet Ami.

"Did you think your brother would marry so soon?" Loki asked Finlay.

"Nay, indeed!" Finlay said. "But I'm happy for him. I hope it works for them."

About two hours later, Maddie and Celestina had set up a large banquet table in the middle of the hall, decorated with greens and ribbons, covered with trays of venison and goose, meat pies, a large pot of lamb stew, brown breads made from rye, barley stew, and mounds of peas and beans. There were also several sweet tarts stuffed with blackberries and cherries.

Loki sat next to Bella and Ami at one of the trestle tables while Kenzie moved back and forth to the door, thrilled with each new arrival. Word had traveled back at Clan Grant, so many had come along to meet wee Ami and celebrate the winter solstice.

Kenzie dashed around the hall, telling anyone who would listen about Father Bor and the orphans. Every once in a while, he would run back toward his parents. "This is just how I wanted it. 'Tis better than having the solstice celebration at the Grants. Do you not agree, Papa?"

After they ate their fill, Loki said, "Kenzie, why don't you find your sack and hand out your packages."

More than pleased to do as his sire asked, Kenzie ran upstairs to grab the enormous sack. When he emerged with it, he announced, "Father Bor explained how he liked to choose a special gift for each orphan and give it out on one eve, the winter solstice. So Papa and I traveled to Edinburgh to choose a gift for everyone."

He made his way around the hall, handing each person a package chosen especially for them. Once he finished, he stood in the middle and said, "Now open them."

He moved back to stand next to his mother to watch her open her gift, declaring, "Look how thick they are, Mama. They'll keep your feet warm this winter."

Bella squealed and said, "I love them. They're perfect." Then she gave him a big hug.

Loki watched the delight on Kenzie's face as he did his best to watch everyone open their gifts: Uncle Alex and Aunt Maddie's tapestry, Aunt Caralyn's special satchel for her healing tools, Uncle Robbie's new dagger, ribbons for Kyla and Gracie, and so on.

When everyone was finished, he stood in the hall and enjoyed his hugs of thanks from everyone. While the others pitched in to help clean up, Kenzie quietly made his way over to his Grandmama. He said, "Now I understand what you meant about giving and receiving love. Giving the gifts was more fun than getting gifts ever is. I hope we can do it again next winter solstice, Grandmama."

"Of course, we will. But are you not upset that you did not receive a gift from anyone?"

He thought about that for a moment and replied, "Nay, 'twas more fun choosing the gifts with Papa." He glanced up at Loki, who smiled down at him. But the lad's smile quickly turned to a frown.

"Papa, I did not get you a gift."

Loki knelt down in front of him. "Think on it, lad. Did we not both receive a few gifts this solstice?"

Kenzie glanced around the great hall and nodded, "Aye, wee Ami and Bor and Fergus and Davina. We are growing, just like you hoped."

Once the hall was clean, the group gathered together near the hearth, moving stools and chairs close by so all of the guests could sit together.

Loki asked for everyone's attention and said, "I finally found out the answer to a question that's bothered me for some time, and I wished to share this with all of you. I've often wondered why I am called Loki instead of Lucas, the name my mother gave me. Father Bor was the one who found me in the woods after I'd been beaten and left to die. He took me to his cottage to help me heal. I would take my anger out on a certain tree, swinging an axe at it as many times as I could. Eventually, I knocked myself out in some way, which made me forget my history. I am the one who named myself Loki after the Norse god. When I came around, I claimed that I, Loki, would make Blackett and Hamish pay for what they'd done to me and to my mother. 'Twas then I traveled to Ayr."

"May I tell them the sad part of our journey, Papa?"

Loki gave him a long look, but then nodded. "Go ahead."

"We stopped in Ayr, where Papa and I both lived in crates. There was a lad who had been living in our crates, but Father Bor found him and took him home because he was sick. The boy died. I understand now that my first mama and papa would never have wished for me to die out there. I know they are glad I was adopted."

No one said a word until Celestina spoke. "Is anyone else aware of Norse mythology?"

"What is that?" Kenzie asked.

"I had to learn about the Norse, and they believe in an entire group of gods that lived many years ago. They say those gods brought the world to what it is today. Is anyone else familiar with their mythology?"

"What does mythology mean?" Kenzie asked.

"Mythology means the study of a group of gods who lived in their own world. In Norse mythology, there is a god named Loki, and we all know that he was considered the wee trickster."

Brodie stood up and announced, "And Nicol and I can attest to the fact that he was a wee trickster when we met him in Ayr." Laughter echoed through the group at this declaration. Loki couldn't help but grin at his adoptive sire. "In fact, he played a few tricks on a couple of evil Norsemen, which is quite fitting, in my mind."

Celestina continued, "Since no one else knows, allow me to explain what I recall. There is a god name Bor or Bors who was the father of Odin and others. Odin is considered to be the father of all knowledge, and he's father to several other gods, Thor being one of them. He also brought the yule, or the celebration of the winter solstice, to the Norse.

"In the myths, Bor was married to a woman named Bestla."

Kenzie jumped out of his chair. "That was her

name. The old woman who took care of the orphans! She was Bestla."

Loki almost jumped from his own chair. "Bor used to tell me tales of the gods, mostly about Thor and Loki. 'Tis why I chose that name. Are you saying that you think Bor and Bestla are gods who came here for some purpose, Mama?"

"Did they ask you to do anything for them?"

"Aye, Bor wants us to take over his life purpose when he goes. He asked if we'd travel to Ayr and Edinburgh at least once a year and bring homeless urchins back to Castle Curanta. To make a home for all the wee ones who don't have families."

Aunt Maddie clutched Uncle Alex's hand. "Oh my, Loki. Many would not believe all you've said, but I do. For my part, I will declare winter solstice to be a time of merriment and gift giving for our clan. Of course, I will assist you with the wee ones at any time.

"My mother was from an area near London, and she believed in the Christian winter holiday of Christmas. 'Tis why we have the decorations and feasting. Now 'tis time to make it an even more special celebration."

Kenzie jumped up and down. "Guess what, Papa? I had another dream last night. I almost forgot it, but Grandmama just reminded me. 'Twas my true papa. He said he was proud of me, and I could love you all forever."

Alex raised his glass and said, "Here's to the yule, for the Norse, the English, and the Scots. To Bor and Bestla and Loki and Kenzie. And to two wee lassies. Abi, whom we'll all meet again someday, and wee Ami, who has found her new home. We'll celebrate together."

Celestina climbed out of her chair and embraced Loki. "That just solidifies something I knew all along. You are a verra special man, Loki Grant. All in the land know it."

THE END

DEAR READERS,
I hope you enjoyed my fanciful tale of Christmas in the Highlands and how it could have all started. This is a complete work of fiction. True, there are Norse gods named Bor and Bestla, but their vocation to care for the wee ones is strictly my creation.

There are stories of Christmas in England during the 1200s but not of the traditional Santa Claus. The tradition of Father Christmas did not arrive until much later in the seventeenth century.

The Norse did participate in revelry for many days around the winter solstice, which is where the term Yuletide developed.

But who is to say where the idea of Father Christmas started?

My world of the Grants and Ramsays does stretch history a bit at times, but I hope only to create more enjoyment.

May all your holidays be as wonderful as Loki and Kenzie's.

Keira Montclair

www.keiramontclair.com

ABOUT THE AUTHOR

KEIRA MONTCLAIR IS THE PEN name of an author who lives in Florida with her husband. She loves to write fast-paced, emotional romance, especially with children as secondary characters in her stories.

She has worked as a registered nurse in pediatrics and recovery room nursing. Teaching is another of her loves, and she has taught both high school mathematics and practical nursing.

Now she loves to spend her time writing, but there isn't enough time to write everything she wants! Her Highlander Clan Grant series, comprising of eight standalone novels, is a reader favorite. Her third series, The Highland Clan, set twenty years after the Clan Grant series, focuses on the Grant/Ramsay descendants. She also has a contemporary series set in The Finger Lakes of Western New York.

Her newest series is The Soulmate Chronicles, historical romance with a touch of paranormal.

84283137R00059

Made in the USA
Columbia, SC
15 December 2017